PEOPLE
OF THE
GROVE

LEE VERN GADSON

Copyright © 2020 Lee Vern Gadson
All rights reserved
First Edition

PAGE PUBLISHING, INC.
Conneaut Lake, PA

First originally published by Page Publishing 2020

ISBN 978-1-64584-637-6 (pbk)
ISBN 978-1-64584-638-3 (digital)

Printed in the United States of America

This book was inspired by a simple short story told to me by a person of simple trusting faith in others and life. Not a blind and unthinking trust but a trust that makes people feel comfortable and welcomed.

Her story was of a chance encounter with a family living in a migrant shack located in an orange grove in East Central Florida back in the 1960s. During a time when ethnic differences were used as a platform for hatred, intolerance, and in some instances, indifference. Back when a nation burned with rage, people rioted in small as well as major cities. When war all but tore the nation apart.

This simple and trusting faith guides the main character of the story, and it leads her into places some fear to go, even today. It also allows her to do wonderful things. It guides her to a place of tolerance and acceptance and finally to true friendship with someone of a different ethnic background

Life lessons are learned and demonstrated by the characters of this book. Lessons we all will do well to emulate.

Disclaimer

Other than the reference to the original story, there are no authenticated facts to this story. The names of towns and places are used only as interpretive reference stances. The story could as well have been set in a citrus grove in Arizona or California; or in a cotton field in Mississippi, Alabama, or Georgia; or in an apple orchard in Oregon, Washington, Vermont, Virginia, or Maine.

Acknowledgments

I thank God for my life and the ability to write this.

I thank my parents who brought me into this world and provided me with great values.

I thank my friend Debbie who gave me the seed for this story.

And I thank you for your support in this.

Although my name is not in lights, I honor my mom with this atonement for the incorrect spelling of my name on my birth certificate. Thank you, spelling notwithstanding, I've always known who I am. My proper name on the title page is for you mom. I love you.

Family in the Grove

This is my story (Debbie, a little girl) as I remember it in Central Florida during the early 1960s, who while discovering who I am as a person and a young lady finds a family of (black) migrant workers living in a citrus grove near my home. The family befriends me, the little girl, and sets me on a new path in life. Dundee, Florida, is a tiny, well-kept town in an agricultural zone founded in 1924. Dundee's population was very small, and most of the people who frequented the town lived in the outlying regions, and although this was the case, most everyone knew each other. Like any place you could think of, Dundee was no exception; rumors of strange events in the town's past were whispered about. Depending on the character of the family talking about it, the conversation took on an in-depth and dramatic nature, or it was glossed over and portrayed as a child's ghost story. Some used the stories to keep the young children in line, to keep them out of the groves and out of trouble with the grove managers. The managers were not happy with people just coming up and taking fruit from the trees; after all any lost product is lost profit. If anyone and everyone living nearby or the northerners driving through on vacation, wanting to take pictures while picking fruit in a Florida orange grove just helped themselves... Well, you can understand that the potential for damage and contamination greatly increase the amount of lost product. There were plenty of roadside juice stands offering all-you-can-drink, freshly squeezed orange, tangerine, white and pink grapefruit juices for a nickel. Except when you asked for more, some of the vendors would sharply reply, "That's all you can drink, 'cause you ain't git'n no more!"

Reason enough to post keep-out signs with penalty of fines and prosecution. The region was a good one. It had a fair amount of topsoil, so farming was possible; there were lakes and ponds on all sides of the little town. This was also good for the animal population. Hunting in the area was good. A north-south road ran to the east of town with a business route through downtown.

Mother said, calling out from the other room, "Don't forget church tonight, and it is your Wednesday-night bath. Also remember when you come home from school stay on the main road, don't cut through the groves. I don't want you near them wild folks in there. You don't want them to get you!"

This was my first day to walk home from school alone. I had been asking Mother for several months now to let me walk home alone. I am nearly a grown lady. Soon I will have my fourteenth birthday; I am nearly a grown lady. Mother has so many chores to do, and she has not been feeling very well lately. Father is gone; Mother says he is on a sales run and that he covers a large territory. I am not sure about that. 'Cause she says he is in Georgia and Alabama. We learned in school that the territories are out west. I ain't say'n she lied to me, but she didn't finish school neither.

"Your ride is here!" Mother yelled out. Mr. and Mrs. Hopper were kind enough to help Mother by giving me a ride to school most days while they were on their way to work. Between chores or if she had business in town, Mother, she would come pick me up or have a neighbor bring me home. That was very kind of them, but I was nearly grown now, and I certainly know my way home.

That day, school was no different from any other day, except I got to walk home alone. I get to be independent! Each moment marked a new milestone for me that day as I anticipated the next moment and finally the end of the school day. Recess came, then lunch, and finally the last period was over. I was so full of excitement that I had to make one last stop at the lady's room.

PEOPLE OF THE GROVE

Finally, it was the end of the school day, and I was on my way. I was walking home by myself. I am independent! The sun was bright that day, the air was fresh and crisp. The wind blew only slightly, and I could smell the perfume of the citrus grove, and I believed I could hear every bird in the trees as I quickly walked away from the schoolhouse.

Suddenly my mind came back to me, and I realized where I was. I had been joined by my friend Billie (a girl). Apparently, she had been going on about some new boy at school. I was not interested, but she was my closest friend, not just at school either. She lives a good piece from me, but after chores we sometimes meet during the weekend and go exploring. We find old farmhouses or places where people say the colored "chain gang" prisoner got his self caught and shot killed. But not in the groves, no, we never go into the citrus grove together. In the summer on Saturday we even meet and go to the creek or one of the lakes to fish and swim some. We always spot moccasins and gators, but they don't bother us none. They like the fish and turtles. One time, Billie caught a tiny bream and this fat ole moccasin came right up along with that fish and just bit down and latched on to that fish, so we both figured it was better that we just let him have it. The hook popped out of the fish's mouth by the time that ole snake got the head around. We joked with each other that as long as the gators didn't try that, we didn't mind.

Billie chimed in and said, "It is very odd not having your mother here with us today or getting a ride home. But I am sure you're glad she is finally letting you walk home alone. After all, you will be hav'n a birthday soon, and no nearly grown lady wants her mom holding her hand in public. Well, this is my road, I'll see you at church tonight I suppose." (She was speaking in a heavy mock Southern accent.)

"Oh! Remember the groves have eyes and every manner of evil in them that likes to git little girls. You know, say there's colored peoples in them groves too that likes to take you and do all kinds of things and they eats you when they is done!"

"Oh you go on with that! You know that was an escaped gorilla that they caught even way before we could hardly walk. But you had better be careful to stay in the middle of the road, 'cause you know how they tell of that giant anaconda snake that stays up in the trees and grabs people who walks too close and swallows them whole.

Billie said, "I ain't scared of no snake, and I certainly will not walk in the middle of the road like some fool escaped retard mental patient. See you tonight at meeting, Deb."

I said, "See you, Billie, and if you don't come to meetin' tonight I'll know why and I will tell your family where to find you."

"So if'n you don't show up we know then that you was invited for dinner…them people's dinner!" Billie said.

Once out of sight of each other, Billie walked in the middle of the road, and me, well, the birds sounded like circling vultures, the wind blowing through the trees taunted me in a way my friend couldn't. But this was our game.

"How silly," I muttered under my breath to myself as I composed myself for the rest of my journey home.

It was several miles from the school to home. Most of the times as me and my mother took the trip, I gave no thought of how far the journey was. But today it was different, and with each step I thought of my independence and how I was growing up.

The thought of walking home quickly faded along with the rhythmic "pat-kerr-swoosh" of my footsteps on the loose clay and sand road. Soon my mind drifts off to a past memory of being in the citrus groves alone nearest to my home and finding a clearing. Perhaps this is where the workers gather to harvest the fruits. There were always some signs of people being there, but I could not remember ever seeing anyone, just some old broken packing crates, several cut-up vehicle tires, and even sometimes old fire burn spots. Once I even found a double-blade pocketknife (with the smaller blade being broken) and an Indian-head nickel and two pennies. The pennies were very odd and old (it was not copper). But at the time of the find they were just odd treasures to be kept.

Since I am close to the place, I might just stop in and see if I can find the workers. (Mother's voice chimes in with her earlier warning from this morning: "Don't go through the groves and stay away from those coloreds that live in there.") Suddenly I realized I was at a place where I figured it was a good place to enter the groves and to get to the clearing where I had found my treasure.

The pat-kerr-swoosh of my steps turned to more of a soft thud as I begin contemplating my actions. One step away from the middle of the road and toward a great adventure, yet one step toward disobeying Mother and yet still one step toward finding more treasure.

After all, soon I will be a grown lady. I should make decisions for myself. How else am I going to learn about the world around me?

Closer to the groves, now Billie's words: "If you don't show up tonight…"

Mother: "Stay away from…"

A new sound in my ears, a thumping pounding sound. My body begins to tremble and shake; my stomach churns.

The first tree is within reach, I think.

I hesitantly and reluctantly retreat; one step toward the middle of the road, I stop then advance toward the trees, then another step in retreat.

No more motherly admonishments in my mind, no more Billie and her "if you don't show up at meeting," less pounding in my ears, even the shakes diminish and no stomach churning. Wahoo! That's better!

Back to the middle of the road. All my instincts and senses return to normal and then I tell myself, "Well, after all I am still a child and I am supposed to do as Mother says!"

The remainder of the walk was uneventful but very contemplative. What if I had gone in and found people, then what would I do? Do I watch them from afar or do I go talk to them? Would they be friendly, or will they eat me? What if they have mean dogs and they attacked me? By the way people talk, they may just have lions and all manner of wild beasts. Did they own the giant snake that got loose all those years back that people speak of? I have never seen a colored in real life. Just some school pictures about the slaves and on television. But on TV everyone and everything is either black or white. I wonder if it comes off? The dark I mean. What do they like to eat, besides people? I wonder if they like grits and eggs and bacon? Do they have birthday parties like me? I am sure they have birthdays, 'cause I am sure they are born, but I guess they do it in the bushes (have the babies, that is).

Mother, I Am Home!

The house smelled of Mother's wonderful cooking, and I could hardly wait to have some of it. Mother came out from the kitchen as I was walking in that direction. We practically ran into each other. She gave me a hug and asked how was my day. I told her all about the lessons in class and how the silly boys acted in class and at recess. I told her about walking partway home with Billie. But for some unexplained reason, I did not mention Billie's and my kidding about the groves. However, my curiosity got the best of me, and I asked Mother a question. That question may as well had been a hot iron dropped on her foot. Immediately she became enraged and began to scold me as if I had done some wrong right in front of her and denied it to her face. All I asked her was if the stories of the giant snake and the colored people in the groves kill'n people was true. I mean to tell you she said that she had better never catch or hear of me ever being in those groves and that I had no business in there. She even reminded me that taking fruit from there was stealing, and she would not hold to that. Then like an eagle swooping down for its prey but as gentle as a mother deer, she took me into her embrace and told me she loved me and that she was afraid for me. She looked me in the eyes and asked if I understood. She leaned forward and gave me a kiss on the left cheek.

I said that I did understand that she worried about me and that I loved her too. Yet I still had a longing to know more of what happened in those groves.

"Now, come on and have a little snack, then you go do your homework and chores. We will have dinner before we go to church tonight."

The afternoon progressed as most other days after school. No phone call from my father nor any messages saying where he was or what he was doing. Mother acted as though she didn't mind. But I could see a little sadness in her face when she stood in the kitchen alone as she looked out of the window as though she saw a thousand miles away or when she was out back at the clothesline, how she would bundle some of the linen and bury her face in them. I am sure she put on a happy face to keep me from worrying and asking too many questions, but I noticed. I will be a grown woman soon after all, and adults must take care of business.

I ate my snack of pimento pepper and cheese spread, milk, and a banana. I've always had a good appetite. Mother says it must all go to my feet, because I was as thin as a rail, as straight as an arrow, and as tall as a beanpole. I finished my chores of collecting, sorting, and cleaning the evening eggs. As usual some had to be thrown out 'cause they were cracked. They became feed for some of the other animals. We could not waist things like I hear people in the city do. We keep around fifty chickens for the eggs and about one hundred to sell to people for eating. We have Porky and Bess; they make piglets for us to sell. Last year Porky had seventeen little ones at one time. That was a record for her. Usually there are between six and nine little ones. The extra ones were welcomed, but it was a lot of work feeding them by hand till they were large enough to eat slop. I even missed some school days. I made up the days I missed by staying at school late for extra credit. Since I plan to attend college, I need to have the best grades possible. Mother plants a vegetable garden for fresh food, and it is all done by hand. We have corn, dried and fresh beans, turnips; we even have celery and lettuce when it is cool…chores all done! Time to clean up for homework (I wonder why they call schoolwork homework, and the work I do at home chores?), and then a great meal.

After the schoolwork and a great meal of roasted pork chops and gravy, mashed potatoes, green beans, and a slice of homemade pound cake, I was feel'n extra energized and ready for the evening. Mother and I cleared the table and cleaned the kitchen and the dishes.

"Go on now, child, get ready for the trip to meeting, and get your sweater. It's gonna be cool on your arms tonight."

We headed out the door and got in the old truck; we have a truck (I call him ole' Buck, 'cause it bounces you around like a wild bucking horse in the movies) 'cause it is more practical than a car. We carry our wares to town to sell to anyone willing to buy, and we also have regular customers. Usually the truck starts without a hitch, but for some reason tonight he strained and moaned, and nothing. We went back inside. Mother called a member of the church but no answer. She tried the church, and still no one answered.

"There has to be something better," Mother said calmly. I suppose that was for my benefit…to show me how to conduct myself in times of adversity. After all, a lady needs to keep herself above reproach, and I will soon be a grown lady.

"You can put your sweater away. We won't be going to meeting tonight. We will read some of the Bible for a bit, and then you can go play for a bit, unless you have more home work to do."

"You mean schoolwork?"

"What?"

"Oh, nothing. Just something I was thinking earlier."

Next Time Billie Alerts Mother

The Baptist church was situated on Main Street, not too many steps from the courthouse and the police department. The building was old but well-preserved. It had been one of the first buildings constructed in the town, and people were proud of it even though no one spoke of it. It was given a washing down every three or four years, depending on how dusty and dry the area had been. A fresh coat of paint about every ten years and everyone turned out to lend a hand. Even the slackers came out and pretended to work, and there was enough incentive for them to do so. There was always a huge spread of food and drinks for everyone who worked on the building. Some came who had not been to church since their wedding or since being baptized. All were invited; all were welcome.

    Tonight, Billie was in her usual place on the side of the church under a grand old oak tree. The place she and I meet before going in. Sometimes Billie is there first like this evening, and sometimes I am there first. But we both understand our ways and wait patiently. On this evening, however, it is different. This was the first time I walked home alone. Sometimes instead of taking ole Buck to pick up us girls, My mom would ride her bicycle and walk with the two of us from school. It was economical she would say…less wear and tear on ole Buck. And what I told her about walking in the middle of the road and getting caught by them killer coloreds. All of these things went through Billie's mind as she waited on me.

What if something has happened to her? I…I can hardly bear to think of it! Mom!

Billie had waited as long as she could, and with the scenes of terror flooding her young mind she could no longer wait for her friend. "Mama! Mama!" (She called in a forceful but quiet voice.)

"What is it child?"

Widowed Mrs. Ida Thornton, Billie's mom. Her husband had passed two years ago. They had been lifelong sweethearts and had grown-up here together. Now he was gone. They say it was the cancer from working in the groves. Him having to use all those chemicals and whatnot. Before his illness and death, he had been a strong, healthy man with a good back, then three years before his passing he just started to dry up; he lost weight. He couldn't or wouldn't eat, unexpected bleeding. The doctors did what they could, but he passed on after that. The doctors figured he had the disease for some time and either was unaware or simply hid it from others. Pride in a working man will cause a person to go through a great deal of unnecessary trouble, be it for good or bad.

Billie approached her mom with quick steps and a discernible look of anguish on her face. This, of course, began to worry her mom.

"Billie! What is the matter? What has got you in such a state, girl?"

"Debbie has not showed up, we always meet under the tree, and she did not come! It is not like her to be this late or to not show up at all! We made plans to meet here tonight!"

"That does not mean something is bad or wrong, child. You know that truck of theirs is old and worn out. It just may be that it won't get to going, or one of them took sick all of a sudden. Besides, they would have called someone. At any rate it is time to go in. We will check on them after meeting if they do not show up. Okay?"

"But Mom, you don't understand! Today was the day Debbie walked home alone. She went all the way by herself, and we talked about that giant snake and the coloreds in the groves. What if something happened? What if they got her? What if she was devoured by the giant snake or them wild people?"

"Nothing like that happened. Those are just stories people made up to keep folks out of the groves. Besides, if Debbie had not showed up at home after school, we surely would know by now. Her mother would have certainly started looking for her with the police's help way before now. Now let's get in our seats…you stay out of those groves, little girl!"

"Yes, ma'am."

It was easier to say "Yes, ma'am" and stop fussing than it was to believe her mom in her mind, but Billie did keep quiet about it. The scene of them walking and teasing each other played over repeatedly in Billie's mind. She could see them walking, and as Billie got to the scene when they parted and I told Billie to walk in the middle of the road and how she had said to me, the colored people would take me and do all sorts of things before eating me.

Billie's discomfort was evident in church, and her mother without fanfare reached over and firmly took hold of Billie's left arm with her right hand and gave her a reassuring squeeze. Billie was sure that at this point if she did not settle down she and her mom would be taking a trip to the lady's washroom for a discussion. So for the remainder of the evening Billie was settled.

The message that night was about "God delivering his people out of trouble."

My mother tried to call again, and still no answer at the church.

I had played out in the yard for a bit. The evening had come on, and I went inside of the house, and my mother and I read the Bible. We read about the people being let out of Egypt and of all the trouble they had during their time in Egypt, as they were leaving and even after they had gone out from there. I understood then how God was with the people in the middle of their troubles and hard times.

No one took notice of time in particular, but time had passed, and then there was a ring of the telephone. It was Billie's mom.

"Hello!"

"Hello, Sara, this is Ida. I called to see how you and Debbie were doing."

"Well hello, Ida. As you see we didn't make it to meeting. I called your house and the church but got no answer. My old truck just would not start. I didn't want anyone worrying about us. I called but no one answered."

"So Debbie is home and well?" (Ida said this as she glared with a playful "I told you so" look at Billie. Billie smiled and so did Ida.)

"That's good. I'm glad you both are well."

"Well, why in the world would you be worried so about Debbie?"

"Today was the first day Debbie walked home alone, wasn't it?" (Ida didn't want to unduly worry Sara, so she just left the rest of it out.)

"Yes, it was and she got home about the time I expected she would. Ida, are you sure that is the only reason for your concern?"

After having just come from church, and knowing she would want to know about her own child, Ida felt she had to answer fully. Well, as the girls walked home, they teased each other about the groves and the stories of the snake and the coloreds. Billie told me if Debbie didn't come to meeting tonight that she would tell us that the colored people living in the groves had taken her and if it was the other way around, Debbie would say the snake had gotten Billie. I guess Billie got herself all worked up over this when you two didn't come to church.

"Debbie didn't say a thi…"—in midsentence, mother remembered what Debbie had asked and brushed off—"she did ask me something about the snake and the colored people. I was a bit short with her when she brought it up. She may have said more if I had not done that. You know, Ida, I think I had better have a talk with Debbie about this and make sure everything is all right. Thanks for calling. Good night now."

"Good night, Sara."

Next Time, Mother and Debbie Discuss the Groves

"Deborah Leigh Rogers!"

My mind wandered off from that present moment…farther and farther.

I have not heard that name in quite some time. In fact I have not heard it in over two years. Only two other times have I been in such a mind-set that I felt I had to be sure I was the correct person in question. I suppose the first time she called me by my full God-given Christian name was after church one fine Sunday, when we went on a picnic over at Lake Ann. There was the three of us then, Mother, Father, and me. It was a fine spring day. It had rained the day prior, so it was not dusty on the old dirt roads. Father looked especially handsome as I recalled; he was wearing a hat, so I could only see the back and sides of his seemingly perfect brown hair. He had removed his suit jacket and tie. His sleeves were rolled up, and I could see his big arm muscles move about as he managed the car's steering wheel. Mother sitting right up next to him seemed to be in another place; she had kind of a thoughtful or pondering look about her. She seemed to bounce up to the roof of the car with every bump in the road. She was so beautiful that day. Her long red hair dropped below her shoulders to about mid back, and blew about as the breeze came into the car windows. At some point she grabbed a hand full of hair twisted it all together, then pulled it around and over her left shoulder then tucked it in her dress at the neck. Still with her expression not changing. After she had pulled her hair over to one side, I could see a mark on her neck. It was kind of yellow-brown with what looked like a little green in it. I reached over and touched it and… and that was the first time I heard that name."

"Deborah Leigh Rogers! You should not be touching a person unawares like that! You could have…" she stopped speaking. At the same moment Father spoke out in a deliberate and pointed way. "Sara!" was all he said. Mother quieted and went back to that look almost before he finished speaking that four-letter name. I forgot about what I saw on Mother's neck, and I thought how Father had just saved me from a tongue-lashing I may have never forgotten. But I did not forget the incident. We made it to the lake, and I can remember a wonderful day of exploring and fishing and eating. That silly old bass, it nearly pulled me into the water, but Father was there to save me. We cooked him right there. The fish I mean.

The other time I heard that name was on a Saturday night, the Saturday night that I will never forget. I had finished my housework. Back then we didn't have many animals, and most of our food came from town. Father worked in town; he was like the second manager of the Feed and Seed store. So I had plenty of time to explore. I told Mother that I was going to play and take a walk to one of the ponds on our property. She just said, "Stay out of the groves." It seemed I had covered all of the county as much as I had walked. I saw all sorts of things. A couple of beavers, an old burned-out car, and I even found a bird's nest with baby birds in it. On the way home I decided to go through the groves. I had never been in there, and all the oranges we get comes from the owner of the Feed and Seed. So I took this road that eventually led to this great clearing. There was no one there since harvest time had passed, and the grass didn't need cutting between the rows. So I went about, first in the middle of the arena, as I called it. Then I spotted this burn area, and in it I saw some old smudge pots. They use these on very cold nights to warm the trees. I looked about more, and I spotted what looked like an old campsite. It had some empty cans: beans, fruits, and the like.

I decided I was going to track the people who were here like the Indians do in the movies and on television. I looked at the ground, and sure enough I found tracks. I found footprints; they were all a jumble, and they went everyplace. So I just started as though I had a good trail. The trail led me to this log; it had been used as a sitting place, I guess. As I approached the log and was looking very carefully for evidence, I spotted a bit of what looked like metal partially buried in the dirt. I reached down and picked it up from the ground, and it was an Indian head nickel. Here I was tracking like the Indians, and I found one; an Indian of sorts, that is. So I looked about more and nothing. So I decided to move the log. It was tough but, I did it and what did I find? A pocketknife. It was already opened. It had two blades, but I could see that the short blade was broken. More coins! Just two pennies. But they looked very odd. The color was off. Oh well, it was my treasure, and I was keeping it. I decided it was way past time to be heading home and so I started walking, then running, and eventually I got home, but it had come night fall. When I neared the house, I could see Mother in the light of the porch.

"Debora Leigh Rogers! That tears it! You should get your little fanny paddled tonight! Just where have you been? I have been worried sick over you! I told you to be in before night fall! You get in that house!"

I expected to hear my dad's voice call out, "Sara!" but there was no voice, and Mother was still going on about how scared she was.

"Get some water and clean yourself up! Are you hungry? Are you okay? Where have you been?"

"Exploring."

I didn't know just what to make of this. Was she angry or was she happy to have me home? Was I going to get a paddling or… wahoo! She scooped me right up with the biggest hug a person could ever imagine or have gotten.

"Mother, I am sorry I frightened you and caused you to worry so."

"It's all right for now, but we will talk about that later. Right now, there is something else that I must talk to you about."

At that very instant I realized that Father had not been anywhere about. And I got a feeling deep in my gut that something had happened.

"Tell me, Mother, what is it?"

"Well, dear, your father is not here. He has gone away. He…he is working for a new company. They sell the products that the Feed and Seed stores sell. So now he goes around selling to the Feed and Seed stores instead of selling to the people. He works in Alabama and Georgia mostly. He also covers a portion of North Florida."

"But when did he leave? Why didn't he say goodbye to me? When will he be back home? Oh! Mother, what are we going to do now?"

"We will continue to live as we have, child. There will have to be some adjustments made, but we will make it just fine."

That's when we increased the number of animals we kept. We even increased the number of operating beehives again, and we did other useful things to support ourselves. Mother bought ole Buck from an even older man who had taken sick and needed the money, since the car had gone with Father.

I never saw another mark on Mother's neck like the one I saw the day we went to the lake, and Mother never had that look on her face of being in a far-off place. The change had been good for her and me too, I suppose. I never did get that talking to nor that paddling that I fully expected and deserved!

Next Time, Conclude Mother and Debbie Discuss the Groves

Mom said, "Listen. Ida just told me you and Billie had some interesting goings-on while you walked home from school. Is that why you asked about the snake and those colored people?"

I replied, "I suppose."

"You suppose? You either know, or you don't! Billie was all in a tizzy after we didn't make it to church. She nearly worried herself into shock."

"It was nothing. We were just having some harmless fun, is all."

"I understand. But when people who care for you are hurt because of your actions, then it is more than harmless fun. Always remember that our actions always have consequences. So before you act, think about the possible consequences. Now why were you asking about the snake and the coloreds?"

"I just wanted to know the truth of the matter. Are the stories real, or are they just to keep us out of the groves?"

"Well, I tend to believe that throughout the total tellings of mankind, there has to be some truth in every story we hear. It's been seen in some of the primitive cultures of the world, and even to this modern day, that some of these people tell stories to share information: about their history, about rival tribes, and about the dangers that surround them. They tell the stories, in some cases, generations after generations, from one storyteller to another, from one tribe to another. They do this 'cause they got no writing. These stories about the grove have been around for so long, I believe no one really knows when they started or who started them. Some of the groves have sold out of the original families' possession, and yet some of the others have been in the same family for longer than I know. I have never met a person who can say they were around when the snake was in the grove. The biggest snake I ever saw from around here was a nine-foot rattler from over near Lake Lanier. Now about killings in the groves, there were these chain gang prisoners that escaped and got in the grove up near little Hamilton, on the southeast side of RT 27. Now this one prisoner got shot while they tried to recapture them. Some say he was colored and he died, some say he just got shot. But everyone agrees on the fact that some colored prisoners were up in those groves. Exactly what happened, I can't say. I was not there.

"Now! As for the colored people living in the groves and killing and eating people. I honestly cannot say, but I do believe that is merely a story and nothing more. I have never seen any Negroes inhabiting those groves, and I have not met anyone who has. I will not share in the dissemination of rumors, even as of the likes of the colored people. Now hear me well, child, do not go rustling about in those groves. It is not safe and it is private property. Do you understand me?"

"Yes, ma'am, I understand you."

But my understanding was one thing, and having my inquisitive nature satisfied was another. I did not want to disobey Mother, but I had a great longing to know what mysteries those groves held for me. I had explored there in part before and I found treasure… except not in this particular part of the groves. I just had to find out about those people for myself. Did they really exist? Do they eat people? Are they naked savages? Where do they come from?

"Mother, I am nearly a grown woman, and I must learn things early in my development lest I be stifled in my mental and educational growth. I have to know the truth about the groves and the colored people. Mother, how many colored people do you know? They never come to town. I have never seen one in person, just on TV and the movies. Do they do all of those things people say they do?"

"Listen, child, they are different from us. They live in the groves, don't they? There are no houses in those groves, and they don't go to town to buy and sell. They certainly don't go to church. These people are just not civilized, if in fact they do live in the groves. I just don't know if these people exist. But I want you to stay out of there just the same. Yes, you are nearly a grown lady, and you do need to experience as much as you can now. But I am still your mother, and it is my duty to teach you as well as to keep you safe."

6

Break—Deb Puts Off Exploring

"Debbie, honey, you take the bicycle to school in the morning from now on if you want. You are old enough now to get to school and home on your own, and I trust you to do so."

I replied, "The truck won't start, and you might need the bicycle in the morning, so I will just walk to school in the morning. I can use it after that to get to school."

"Good idea! Now off to bed for you. Good night, honey."

"Good night, Mother!"

It was somewhat of a restless night. The anticipation of getting to school all by myself and the thought of the strange people that may live in the groves ran through my mind over and over. But even this was not greater than the power of the sandman.

The next morning arrived. I was filled with anticipation and bolted upright in bed and in the same motion flew to the floor in a full-out run to clean up and get dressed for school. Breakfast was already being placed on the table, and just about the time Mom called for me to come down to eat, there I was in place and ready to begin.

"Good morning, Mother."

"Good morning, dear, how did you rest?"

"Mostly on my side, and you?"

This brought a big smile to Mother's face, then she replied, "Oh, about the same."

"Now you eat up, then off to school you go."

"Yes, ma'am! This sure looks good, and I am hungrier than a flathead catfish after a long winter."

"Now you remember what we talked about last night, and you be careful as you go. I certainly hope ole Buck isn't completely dead. I'd hate to have to go out and buy another truck."

"Yes, Mother, I will be careful. And if any strangers come near me, I will take out my pouch of salt in case I need to protect myself. Then I will run as fast as I can."

I did not want to alarm Mother, so I didn't say all that was on my mind I'd do in the event the incident I had just described did occur. Which was to run into the groves. Where else would I run? After all, the roads between school and home were long and barren. That salt to the eyes would not have a very long period of discomfort. I simply would have no other choice if it came to that.

"Take your raincoat and here is your lunch. Do you have your homework?"

"I have my schoolwork, and I will do my homework this evening when I get home."

The morning air was fresh and crisp. Birds could be seen and heard near and far. Mom had thought it might rain, but unlike the low red sky of an impending rainy day, these clouds were very high in the sky, and they were as white as freshly washed pillowcases. A rabbit dashed across the road in front of me, but before it completed its journey, it stopped, sat up-right upon it's hind feet, and glanced my way, as if to bid me a good morning. All this served, at least in my mind, to assure me that I would have a good day. The remainder of the trip to school was as pleasant but uneventful. As I neared the schoolyard, I could see Billie sitting on a bench alone. Billie had her back toward the direction that I approached from. A perfect position to scare her. The raincoat! I quickly rolled it lengthwise as I neared. Then at just the right moment as I stretched out my arm with the coat, the bell rang and Billie jumped up to walk off.

"Billie! Wait up!"

"There you are. I waited and waited. I thought you weren't going to show up. Did your mom get the truck fixed? Or did she fix your wagon?"

"We will talk about it at recess. How about you?"

"Yeah, it's a long story…okay, recess then."

The morning classes were as they always are. The class clown was in attendance, that would be Robbie Johnson. Freddie liked Samantha so he pulled her hair and wrote her notes. Notes that she "tore up" but never threw away in the class trash. Then there is the teacher, Mrs. Dean, she reminded me of Mother. She was very understanding, but she could be strict and firm if she had to. The next class was the same as the first and so was the last. We had a small school, so there was no need to go from one room to another. The only difference was that the teachers changed and the subject changed. We had Miss. Steinholtz for math and history. All the teachers took turns monitoring recess, which doubled as physical activity. There were about fifty children in the whole school and three classrooms. Even Mrs. Turner, the principal, taught one of the subjects, and she was the head substitute teacher. She was mean. At least everyone thought she was mean. She never smiled. When she had business with a student, she would look over her glasses and down at you. If this was not intimidating to someone, they were not alive.

Next Time the Girls Talk about What Happened

Recess could not come soon enough for the both of us girls. But at last it was that time, and we headed out of the classroom with an unwavering determination. Several people tried to get our attention but were met with an "I've gotta go!" "Talk to you later" or even "See you after school." Finally we arrived at our spot, away from everyone.

Billie said, "Momma…"

I replied, "Mother…"

We both tried to speak at the same time, which produced a small giggle from us both.

I told Billie to go first, but Billie said, "No, you go 'cause you didn't come to church. Just in case you are not around much longer."

But I said, "It will be a better story if you went first, that way I can fill in the blanks for you. Anyway, Mom and me read the Bible, so I am okay."

Billie agreed.

Billie said, "So I got home from school, whole and alive. No snakes in the grove to devour me. I did see a snake run across the road ahead of me, I believe it was a coachwhip. That unnerved me a bit. Not because I saw him, but 'cause it made me think of the other all the more. Even the middle of the road didn't seem safe enough at the time. When I arrived at home my mom reminded me to do my chores and homework..."

I said, "You mean homework and schoolwork."

Billie replied, "Huh!"

I said, "Nothing, I'll explain later."

Billie said, "She had made me a peanut-butter-and-banana sandwich and glass of milk. After all of my work was finished, it was time for supper. We had a feast for a Wednesday. And I am so glad it was not my 'last supper.'"

We both smiled. I interjected, "A bit off cue, but that was good."

"After we ate and cleaned up, we got in the car and drove over to the church. I waited under the oak, but then you didn't come and I had to go inside. I told my mom about our talk when I just couldn't hold back no longer. I was worried 'bout you. Momma even put the squeeze on my left arm. Wanna see?"

I said, "Sure!"

Billie rolled up the sleeve of her dress to expose a perfect thumb mark on the inside of her upper arm. She held her arm up and another finger or thumb mark on the inside.

I said, "Wow! You must have been worried about me for her to do that!"

Billie replied, "Well, with all the talk of giant snakes and wild colored people on the loose, I just could not sit still. Anyway, Mama said she would check on things after church."

I said, "So my mother did know the whole story when we talked later. We were finishing up reading the Bible, and the telephone rang. Mother answered and talked to your mom. My mother talked about the truck not starting and me asking about the things in the groves. She didn't say how she had gotten upset with me about the groves."

Billie said, "She got angry with you? What did she do? Did she put the squeeze on you?"

I replied, "Nooo, she did not put the squeeze on. But she did get angry, and she told me in so many words that the groves were not my business. But after the conversation on the telephone, she seemed to have a change of heart. We had a long conversation, and she told me all she knew about the groves. The bottom line is that no one really knows if the story about the snake or the coloreds living and eating people in the groves are real. But the shooting of the chain gang prisoner did happen. Whether or not he was killed is another matter."

"I wonder what made her change her mind and tell you those things?"

"I suppose she realized that I will soon be a grown woman, and I need to know things so I can be better prepared for life."

Billie said, "My mom says that I will always be her baby and that I am all she has that is good. I love my mom, even after she put the squeeze on me."

I began to speak.

I said, "Well, I'll tell you…"

The class bell rang to bring the conversation to a halt.

"I'll tell you later."

Next Time on the Way Home

The remainder of the school day went, it seemed to us girls, very slowly. But the final bell rang eventually, and we were on our way out the door and down the road.

I commented, "I felt like everything moved in slow motion. I thought it would never end."

Billie replied, "I felt like I was holding my breath and coming up from the bottom of Lanier but never reaching the surface, yet having it in view."

"Finally, everything is moving at a normal speed for me and you've reached the surface."

"So now what, Deb?"

"What do you mean, Billie?"

"Well, I guess I mean, what are you going to do about the groves? Are you going to go in there and explore like you figured?"

I replied, "I haven't made up my mind yet. Mother does not want me to go in there, and even though she has talked to me about what to do if a stranger tries to git me on the way home, she never said to run into the groves to get away. Now, Billie, you know there's no place to hide except in the groves. Sometimes I think she and other grown-ups try to pretend that the groves are not there. How can you avoid them? How can you deny them? Well, I can't! But I don't want to disobey my mother either."

Billie replied, "You may just be better off if you just forgot about the groves too. It sounds like trouble all around to me."

I said, "How does it sound like trouble to you? Tell me what you mean!"

Billie replied, "Well, first on the easy side of it all, if you get caught in there by the manager or the police you will be in big trouble for just being there. Your mom will be plenty upset with you. But at least you would be home, in trouble nonetheless, but home safe. If you stay out of the groves you can be home safe any way and not have your mom be angry with you. Now another point is, if you go and you find the people in there, what if they kidnap you and… and do all of those sordid things people say they do to people. Then what? Your mom will be sad, and I will just simply die if something like that happened to you. We will never see you again. Never mind about the snake, the gorilla, or chain gang prisoners."

I said, "That's certainly a bucketload to carry. I see your point of view. But I feel something inside of me urging me onward. It's as if I got something inside of me that just has to get out, and I can't stop it from forcing me. You know how you feel come Christmas time. You know the gift under the tree is yours, but you just got to know what's in it. Well this is ten times stronger than that. They say the earth and the moon have magnetic attraction to one another. The moon pulls on the earth, and the earth pulls back. That is me and them groves. But there is the sun shining bright, lighting up the day and heating the earth. It is bigger and stronger than both the earth and the moon put together, that's the pull of finding the colored people in the groves has on me. I just gotta know about them! You see, Billie, I've been in parts of the grove before, and I had fun learning in it, but I have never seen any colored people in real life. There is something inside of me asking a question, a question that I don't understand at the moment. I have to find the question and then the answer. That is just the way of things!"

Billie said, "Well all I can say is, it's sure a good thing that you will soon be a grown woman. 'Cause if you survive this, your mom will kick you out of the house. So now what?"

I replied, "Now nothing, I guess. The way I figure it, I have to think on it some more and then see what happens. No sense rushing into this thing. Well, this is your turnoff. I guess I will see you in the morning at school."

Billie said, "Yeah, this is my road. Hey! Why don't we try to time it so we meet here, and that way we can walk together?"

I said, "You know I have to do some chores before I leave the house, but that is a great idea. Tell you what. Whoever gets here first waits for ten minutes, if the other person does not show up, write a note in the sand on the side of the road. This will let the other person know that they are last. We don't want to be standing around here all day."

Billie replied, "Great idea! See yah!"

"See yah!"

Next Time Smell of Food (Passing Grove)

The walk home was different somehow for both of us girls. There was no anticipation of danger or images of terrible things occurring from within the grove. The sun was bright and the air warm. It had the scent of fresh-tilled soil. The workers and tractors could be heard way off in the distance by Billie. As she walked toward home, the sounds got louder. It was a familiar sound. Fertilizer being dropped and tilled into the soil before the next bloom. The tilling also cuts down weeds and unwanted grasses near the trees. Billie could smell water in the air also. The irrigation had been turned on in the areas that had been prepared already. Although none of this could be seen by Billie, she could visualize it all. *Perhaps the section near the road I am walking on will be done tomorrow or perhaps tonight after I've passed,* she thought.

As I walked, I began to think of the work I had to do at home and what I would have for supper… Collect the eggs, feed the animals, water the animals, check for baby animals, check for dead animals. I thought how nice it would be this weekend when me and Mother would collect honey from the hives we kept.

Mother's dad kept bees. For all of her life she had bees and other animals around. That is why she is so good with them. When they are sick, she knows just what to do. When the babies come, she knows just what to do. When they die, she knows what to do then too. She preserves the food from them, she tans the hide from some of them. You know, I guess she can just about do anything she want to with those animals 'cause she learned how when she was young. Well, I am going to learn what she knows and then more.

My mind floated over to dwell on supper.

Leftovers from last night's meal I think. Mother has never made a bad meal. She will transform the pork into a casserole or a stew, or she may make one of her special sandwiches.

Just then my stomach groaned as if to say, "I am hungry," but why had it done that? As my mind cleared from the anticipation of this evening's potential events, I realized why my stomach had growled so. I could smell the unmistakable aroma of something cooking. It smelled great. This made me all the more hungrier.

Hush up! You'll get fed soon enough! My thoughts went straight to entering the groves to discover just who, or what, was in there. I had never stepped more than a row or two into this part of the grove, and I had only a guess as to how large it really was. I tried to picture the lakes in the greater surrounding area and then picture where I was in relationship to this part of the grove. I knew people would need to be near water. They will need it to cook with and drink and wash clothes and bathe (if they do laundry and bath). The aroma of burning wood intermixed with whatever was being cooked, and my own passion was very compelling, so much so that I had, without realizing, walked right up to the first row of trees. I reached out my left hand as if to steady myself against a raging battle within myself. Go in! No! Mother said… With a light push off and a step away from the trees, I was on my way home. Just as quickly as I had made the decision to not go into the grove, so was the aroma of food as quick to disappear. With several deep sniffs of the now-familiar air and thoughts of what it could have been. I quickly moved off from the grove and headed home. I quickened the pace even more, and before I knew it, my feet and body kept pace with my very active mind, and I was running.

Next Time Home with Mother

It seemed only a moment ago that I was at that tree in the grove, but now I was in the yard. Home safe once again.

M...o...th...errr! I'm home! M...o...th...errr! There was no answer. I moved through the living room toward the kitchen where I usually found mom. There was only silence. No pots clanging. No sound of whistling, bubbling, or boiling on the stove. Sure enough, the kitchen was empty. But there was a note on the table.

"Debbie, change clothes, then get a snack. You may have anything you like, just not too much. Then come out to the hives. I will explain later. Love, Mother."

Oh great! Last night it was the truck and now it's the beehives. I'll just change clothes and grab an apple and a cookie. I'll have it as I am on my way to the hives. I wonder what the problem is and how many hives are affected.

On the way to the hives, I saw a skunk family; it looked like a mother and two kits. They moved off fast when they saw me nearing. To me they were suspects, and a slight bit of contempt arose in me for them. The hives were in six locations along the border of a section of the groves to the northwest of the house, and each set contained ten hives, paired in twos on their platforms. This way a person would not have to walk around a single row of ten hives. It made it easier to work. They had been here for years and years. This was Grandpapa's place, about one hundred acres. And the hives were his, although

Mother had replaced some of the older ones, and there used to be many more than we have now. We used to have someone help with the hives on a regular basis, but now that I am able to help Mother, she did not need the extra help, except when she does what she calls destabilization prevention rotation. That happens when a hive begins to swarm. When a queen bee leaves the hive, she takes worker bees with her. If there is no queen bee left in the hive, it has no one to care for it then, and the hive dies. That rarely happens, though, but Mother said she'd rather be vigilant than sorry. We take the swarming queen and install her into another hive and start a new colony. Most times we get two for the price of one. Mother says the sales of the honey is my college fund. So I am working my way through college now. She even sells the wax to cosmetic companies. Between them and candlemakers, Mother sells all the bee products we have. Some of the buyers ask her over and over to expand. They even say they will provide her more hives and bees. They say she can even rent her bees to the citrus growers as pollinators. Mother says it would be too much to deal with on a daily basis, and if she allows others to join us, they may eventually try to take our business and Grandpapa's land. But she doesn't tell them this, of course. She just politely declines their offer.

Next Time Hive and Seek

As I approached one of the stands, I noticed what looked like fresh tire tracks. As I continued to approach the hives, I looked for damage and evidence of tampering. Mom was not there, so I quickly moved on. I proceeded from the clearing that contained the hives, on to the small road we maintained. After a short walk, I could hear the bustling and buzzing of people and bees. "Mother!" I called out several times. Mom had taught me to call out when approaching a campsite or people you can't see. Frightened people and animals may hurt you, but if it is a dangerous animal they will usually move off. I rounded the small turn in the road and stand of trees. To my horror, several hives were set askew on their platforms, and one was even knocked over. Bees were everywhere. I knew I could not approach safely, and if the bees sensed me, I would be done for before I could reach help. I had no idea how far off Mom was. I wrapped my long-sleeved shirt around my head and moved in as close and quietly as I dared. I stopped, and just then I heard a loud crash from the woods that backed the groves, and I thought I saw the figure of a person. I moved back slowly and headed toward the next stand. This time with a greater sense of urgency, I picked up the pace. As I neared the next set of hives, I was certain it was Mom. Someone was with her. I heard talking and the door of a vehicle slam shut. I had not thought about Buck till I heard the door close. I ran faster. I reached the truck just as Mom was starting it up. Waving my hands and yelling, I got Mom's attention.

"Mother! Mother!"

Mom opened the truck door and exited. A greeting and somewhat confused look on her face quickly turned to that of concern.

I said, "Mother! Someone has damaged the second set, and I thought I saw someone in the woods behind the hives."

We two met at the rear of the truck and was quickly joined by old Mr. Knowles who is part Indian and has been living here since birth. He is called Hoot. He is called this, because when he was a young boy, he and his older brother and father were on a fishing trip on Lake Hamilton, and as they sat near the fire one night, he called out in response to the hoot of an owl. After several exchanges a young owl swooped down and lit on his head. Even as a boy he was not frightened and took this as a great honor. From then on he was known as "The one who calls owls" or "Hoot."

Mom said, "Are you all right, Debbie? Did any bees get you? Let me check anyway. Why, with all the excitement you may not even feel the stinger in you."

"Hello, Debbie. She is right," interjected Hoot. "After the excitement wears off, if you are severely stung you could succumb to the venom from the stingers. She should check now."

"Hello, Hoot. I feel fine. Also, I think I saw shoe prints at the second set of hives. I am sure they were not yours. They sat deeper and was larger. They also seemed to circle the hives. Your prints approach toward the entrance, and they get mixed up as you shift your weight from you opening the caps."

Hoot replied, "You are a good tracker, young one!"

Mom said, "Okay! All done. No stingers here. Now let's go see about those hives."

It seems Mother is never shaken by anything, except for when it comes to me. It is as if she nearly falls apart if there is an issue with me. Me knowing about the people in the grove for example. "Thank you, Hoot, and you too, Mother! Have the other hives been checked yet?" I said.

Hoot said, "No, they have not."

I said, "Mother, I think we should see about them first. If someone is heading to those hives, we might just scare them off. And the affected hives are not swarming so the bees will stay put anyway. The damage, if any, to the hives is done already."

Mom said, "Very good thinking, Debbie. Hoot, you ready?"

Hoot stood motionless and in silence, looking toward the tree line.

Mom said, "Hoot!"

"Yes! Yes, I am. I was listening and looking to see if there was anyone out there. I sense nothing."

I said, "Thank you, Mother. But after all, I am nearly a grown woman."

I was set to ride on the tailgate.

Mom said, "No, no! You come ride in the cab with us. I want to make sure you are okay if anything happens."

See! I am not just imagining things. She just goes to pieces. Hmmm, I thought.

The ride was quick, if not smooth. A quick check of the fourth set and off to the remaining two sets. We found no evidence of tampering, and even as important, no swarming. So back to the place of the incident.

As the truck approached the set, it stopped farther away than usual. If the bees were agitated, the truck would be their target, and we would lose many bees unnecessarily. We would also have to suit up to get to the hives.

The three of us sat for a moment looking and assessing the hives for activity out of the usual. Even though the hive was upset, the worker bees continued to provide for the hive as programmed. The guards stayed on alert. But it looked as good as it gets. We slowly and calmly exited the truck, pushing the doors shut as quietly as possible.

After a few moments of silent assessment and calm…

Hoot said, "Ah! It is as you say, little one. There was one person here. The soles of the shoes are smooth and worn. They leave no other prints. The tracks circle then approach from the rear. Here, see how deep the prints here are? That is when the hive was pushed over. The increased pressure or weight made the heels dig deeply into the earth at this point. Then, perhaps that is when you approached little one. The tracks head off into the trees here."

I said, "Yes, that is about right. When I heard the crashing and buzzing about, I called out so as to not startle you. Just like you taught me, Mother."

Mom said, "Just as Hoot taught me." He smiled.

Hoot said, "We all learn if we keep an open mind and a willing heart."

Mom said, "Well, Hoot, it all looks as if it can be salvaged without difficulty."

Hoot replied, "Yes. A bit of caution is required, however. We will smoke the bees then set the hive upright and then back onto the platform."

Mom said, "I will get the things we need for that. Debbie, you get the extra frames from the box. We won't know how many we will need. Please get the bucket for the combs. If the combs are broken, and I am sure they will be, we won't be able to carry them in the boxes. We will have to use the honey for ourselves. We can still sell the wax."

Hoot said, "The hive is intact! Hoot called to affirm that the queen was alive, as well as in place. One comb broken!"

Mother and I looked up in great surprise. Hoot had sat the hive upright and managed to open the cap and find the queen in just a matter of seconds. The hive was calm even after all this.

We exchanged the one grid without smoking the bees. The three of us repositioned the overturned hive on its platform, sat the askew hives aright and not one bee sting among the three of us.

Next Time Back to the House and Who Could It "Bee"

Mother allowed me to ride on the tailgate on the way back home. The ride was very slow. Our truck still lived up to its nickname: "Ole Buck." After the earlier events, I felt I could use a little distraction, so I pretended the bouncing ride of the truck was a ride at an amusement park or the fall carnival. Soon we were back at the house. Everyone exited the truck, taking something with them. We each put the item we carried in the processing barn. We placed the honeycomb near the small extraction bin Mother used only for honey that we would not sell. Using a smaller piece of equipment helps with the cleanup after the extraction process. But this time there was only one honeycomb to process. Mother cut the caps over the cells of the comb and placed the pieces over a screen, which angled down in a cone shape, and she just let the honey run out of the comb pieces on their own. She had been busy; I had never seen this thing before. We cleaned all of the other things and placed them in the clean area of the barn.

"Hoot," Mother called out, "give me a moment."

She went to the back room of the barn, and after a brief moment she returned with some money and a jar of honey for Hoot.

"Thank you for your help. I will never know how you knew that our hives were in danger, but I am so very glad you came by to tell me."

Hoot said, "Having an open mind and willing spirit allows us to hear nature speak to us. The spirit uses many things to talk to those who will listen."

Mom replied, "Well, thank you again for listening and heeding nature's voice. You saved us more than we can know? Would you like a ride?"

"No. I will walk. I have no place to be in a hurry."

I said, "Mother, may I walk with Hoot a little? I would like to talk with him a bit."

Mom said, "Okay, but don't go far and don't keep him long. You still have work to do!"

I said, "Thank you!"

Hoot clutched his honey close to his left side and put the money away in his right pants pocket. The two of us walked out of the barn. The sky was still bright, although the sun could not be seen for the surrounding trees.

Hoot said, "How may I help you, little one?"

I said, "Hoot, you have lived here longer than anyone else I know. Can you tell me about colored people living in the groves? Is it true? I have never seen a colored person before. I want to see what they look like."

Hoot said, "Debbie, do you remember my words? If you have an open mind and willing heart. First, understand that you have seen a colored person. As you stand before one now. I am part white and part Indian, true, but colored nonetheless, although not Negro. Next thing is to understand that a man is a man. No matter the color of his skin. Now if you ask the question, is he a good man or is he a bad man, you will have to understand his heart to know that, and you must get to know him to understand his heart. Think of this, look at the birds. Are they all the same? The meadowlark has his colors, the robin has his colors, the eagle his, the turkey his, the blackbird and the red-winged blackbird their separate colors. Then think on this, little one, some fly high as the eagle and some below the eagle, but some barely get off the ground as the turkey. All birds—all beautiful in its own way and useful in nature. People are this way also. This is the way of nature. This is the way the great creator has put things."

I replied, "Then it is true! They live in the groves. Have you seen them for yourself? Did you speak with them? Do they talk like us?"

Hoot replied, "Yes. All true."

I said, "But why? Why do they live in there away from everyone?"

"Think on this, little one. Ponder all of my words from this day...an open mind and willing heart. The birds of the field and air. Some birds eat seeds, and some eat flesh. Some birds fly in the open and some under cover of the trees. Reflect on how you noticed the shoe prints at the hives and how you cared for the bees. When you understand these things, then you will have your answers. Return home now, you must not worry your mother."

I said, "I don't understand! You don't look colored to me."

Hoot replied, "And with that you have the beginning of understanding. Go! Ponder!"

I returned to the house as quickly as possible, knowing schoolwork still had to be done as well as any homework Mother felt needed to be done was going to be there still.

Mom had finished in the barn and returned to the kitchen to prepare the evening meal.

Mom said, "Debbie! Are you hungry? With all of the excitement, I thought we would take a moment to eat and talk. So you go wash up and come back to the table. Okay?"

I replied, "Okay!"

There was left over potato salad and a piece of fried chicken along with some roast beef. There had been what was described as the best peach cobbler ever made in the fridge also. Cold milk or iced tea were the choices of drinks. Everything was in place when I returned to the table.

Mom said, "You say grace, please."

I replied, "Yes, ma'am. Thank you, Lord for the bounties of our labors and your grace. May this food nourish us to your honor. Remember those who are not as fortunate and the Ni...Negro people in the groves. Thank you for Hoot. Thank you for Mother. Amen."

Mom said, "Amen. Debbie, why did you pray for the colored people?"

I replied, "I don't know, I just did. They were on my mind, and it just came out."

Mom said, "And why were they on your mind, young lady? Have you been in those groves?"

I replied, "No, ma'am." (I attempted to deflect with silence.)

Mom said, "No, ma'am what? 'No, ma'am, I have not been in the groves' or 'No, maa'm, I am not going to tell you?'"

I replied, "Mother, I have not gone into the groves. I just thought of those people being out there, and I got to wondering about who they are and how they may live. I think are they like us or are they so much different?" (Without thinking and not pausing, I expelled some of the teachings of ole Hoot).

"Look at the different kinds of birds in the world, Mother, they have their differences, and they seem to get along and they fly at different heights. Some high like the eagle and some low like the turkey or our chickens. They are different from each other, but they all are birds."

Mom replied, "I see. You are just wondering about other people. Well, let me tell you, I worry about your safety. You are all I have, and I don't want to lose you. I know you are growing up, and there will come a day when I will have to let you go. That day is not today. Do not go into the groves looking for those people! After we finish here, you go do your homework, and if there is any light left you can water the side garden and collect the evening eggs. We don't want the hens to stop laying. Try not to be very late, they will get off cycle, and we will have to collect later and later each day."

I replied, "Yes, ma'am. Mother, have you thought about what happened to the hives today? Who could it have been?" (Even at the risk of Mom getting angry, I brought up one possibility of who could have done the mischief at the hives). "Do you think the Negroes could have made their way over to the hives? I did see a family of skunks, a mother and two kits."

Mom said, "I am sure the skunks had nothing to do with it. As for the colored people, I doubt it, but you never know."

I thought, *Mother almost defending them! Not knowing who did it and nearly excluding them from the incident seemed a bit odd. Who else could it be?*

Neither of us spoke another word till all tasks were completed and we had prepared for bed.

Mom said, "Debbie, I am so proud of how you handled yourself today, and you pray for whoever you want to. I love you, good night."

I replied, "I love you and thanks. Good night. Oh! What was the problem with Buck? How did he get fixed?"

Mom said, "A funny thing, the battery terminal connection was loose…so loose, in fact, that it was ready to come off in my hand. Hoot showed up as I was heading out to look at the truck. He helped me find the problem, and afterward we went to check on the hives. He said he felt uneasy about them. You know the rest. Good night."

Next Time, Not Just Another Day

The next day began as most days: get up, put on clothes, do chores, come back inside, clean up and change clothes, have breakfast, do some planning with Mother, and off to school.

Mom said, "Are you taking the bicycle today? It will help you get to school faster."

I said, "I really enjoy walking, but I think I will."

Mom said, "Your lunch is all ready, here you are."

"Thanks, Mother!"

"Do you have your raincoat? Did you check your safety pouch? Is it dry?"

I replied, "I have the coat, and a few grains of rice keeps my safety pouch nice and dry!"

"Then off you go!"

"Bye!"

The bike ride was not new to me. At one time we had two bicycles, but one was stolen and never recovered. Me and Mom had ridden to town and to school on them on many occasions. Until now I have not ridden alone. But Mom trusted me, and I realized I had to grow up. To do this, I had to learn to make good choices for my life. Mom knew I could not learn to make the proper choices unless I was given some freedom to do so.

The ride was at a nice leisurely pace, and yet far faster than I could walk. So I was ahead of schedule. I realized I would likely have to wait for Billie. I thought of what I would write if I had to leave before Billie came. I thought of how nice the day was. Then I thought back to yesterday. I thought of Ole Buck not starting, the hives, the shoe tracks at the hives. I also thought of my talk with Hoot. What could this mean? It has been over a year that the other bike was taken. Can the incidents be related?

"I know! When I get back home, I will follow up on an idea."

At that moment I came to the junction where me and Billie go our separate ways to get home. There was Billie just a few yards away from the intersection. We waved at each and called out.

Billie yelled, "Hey!"

"Hey!"

"Wanna ride with me?"

"No! Let's walk."

"Okay!"

I said, "Put your stuff in the rear basket, no need to carry them now."

"Thanks!"

"How is your mom, Billie?"

"She is fine. She had a small bout of rheumatism. But after a hot bath and some of her medicine, she felt better. She got up this morning and fixed me a feast for breakfast. My lunch feels extra heavy too. What about your mom?"

I replied, "She is well. Something or someone got into the hives. One was turned over and several others were upset. We managed to save everything though. I believe I saw someone in the woods behind the damaged hive, and I did find shoe prints at the hives. I found Mother and Hoot at another location checking hives. I told them what I had found, and we all went together to see. We don't know who it was, but we all agree that it was a person and not an animal."

Billie said, "Deb, how can you know for certain that it was a person?"

I replied, "Except for the traveling circus, bears in this part of the state are unheard of. They have them in the Everglades and even up around Tampa but not here. Besides, bears don't wear what look like size-ten shoes. Even if the others are not certain of it being a person, I am."

Billie said, "Okay then, just what are you going to do about it? You don't know who it was, you don't know where the person came from, nor where they went. I hope you don't try to camp out at the hives overnight alone. Oh! By the way, I am not volunteering to camp out with you if you decide to do that."

I replied, "I don't know yet what to do. All I know is that if it happened once, it will happen again, and I must find out who it is and why they did that. I will figure out something."

Billie said, "Oh yeah, before I forget completely. My mom would like a big jar of honey, a dozen eggs, and two big roasters for Sunday dinner."

I replied, "I will tell Mother. She will deliver on tomorrow, with the other drops she has to make."

Billie said, "That sounds good. Will you be with her?"

"I should be. There is nothing special going on. Why?"

"Oh, I just thought we would get to see each other and spend a little time together."

"Well, I will see if Mother can spare me for a bit, and maybe we can spend a hour or two together. But you know she tries to sell as much as she can on Saturdays."

Billie said, "Just see what she says and don't forget the honey and the black legs."

At the mention of black-legged chickens, I instantly began thinking of the people of the groves and the overturned hive. In my mind this gave me another reason to enter the groves. I not only felt a need to explore the groves, but now I had a cause; I must investigate to determine what happened to the hives. As suspects, I had eliminated the furry skunk family, but now I felt I may have another family of skunks to deal with.

You could travel unseen for miles and miles through those woods and groves. Perhaps this was how the person got to the hives unseen. We searched for tracks at the hive heading into the woods away from the place of the disturbance, but what if we missed tracks coming in across our property? A person living off the land is one thing, but if you have a whole family living off whatever they can find and not caring if it belongs to someone else, then that could be awful.

Billie said, "Debbie! Debbie! Do you hear me in there?"

"Huh! What!"

"Just as I thought, you were off on one of your mind adventures, weren't you?"

"You know, I think I have an idea as to how that person got to the hives. I'm going to investigate it after school today. I am going to get to the bottom of all of this business, then we will know just what happened and who got into those hives. We might even find out why!"

Billie said, "Well, whatever you have planned, you just make sure you get my mom's chicken and honey on that truck. Here let me get my things out of the basket. Did you bring a lock and chain for your bicycle?"

"No. I didn't. It should be okay here at the school."

"I guess. Let's get on the swings. It looks like we are early."

"Okay! Hey, did I tell you I saw a family of skunks on the way to the hives? There were three of them crossing the road, a mom and two kits. They were so cute. I think they wanted to stay as far away from me as I wanted to stay from them, and they hurried off into the trees. You know, when I saw them, I thought this might be the reason Mother was at the hives and had left me the urgent note. It turned out to be something different altogether. Billie, do you ever blame somebody in your mind for something even before you know all of the facts? They were only skunks, but I had blamed them and I begun to dislike them at that moment."

Billie replied, "I suppose I do. But what of it? Just 'cause you think something in your head don't mean a whole lot, I guess…that is until you do something."

I said, "Yeah, but what if what you think causes you to act in a certain way, and you cause harm to an innocent person? You know, I don't think I would like myself very much after something like that."

Billie said, "You can always say I'm sorry."

I replied, "I don't think it is just that simple, Billie. *Sorry* is like an ole hound that won't bark and let thieves take what you have. It does no good."

Billie replied, "It makes people feel better after you say it. Doesn't it?"

"Yes, but who really feels better, the person hearing it or the person saying it? After all, the person saying it was not wronged or otherwise harmed."

"I see your point. What are you thinking?"

I said, "Oh! I had a conversation with Hoot, and it just got me to thinking in other terms."

"Oh! Well, you…"

The school bell rang.

I said, "A deep subject for such a shallow mind."

Billie replied, "At least it is a 'gold mind.' What do you have? Oh! I know…skunks!"

I said, "You win this time!"

The remainder of the school day was fairly routine. Classes proceeded as usual, and notes were passed for my mother to fill orders. Some were for deliveries, and some were for pickups at the truck on the side of the road. Route 27 gets pretty busy with the weekend travelers. This usually sells an extra case or two of honey on Saturday. So the day ended. The girls headed to the bicycle, which was nowhere in sight.

Did we leave it here? I thought. I was certain of it.

Billie said, "Oh! Debbie, I am so sorry!"

Just as Billie said that, my thought reverted to the conversation of this morning. I gave Billie one of those stares that usually only a mother could give. And just as quickly I broke and smiled.

Billie said, "It's okay. Everything will be all right."

Billie just could not contain herself any longer; besides, they had to get home and they could not afford to linger at school long.

Billie said, "Your bike is over there, tied up. I borrowed a cable and lock from Mr. Carver." (He was the groundskeeper, among other things, which included bus driver, janitor, maintenance man. Whatever needed done that did not involve teaching, he is the person. When it came to the school cookouts, he handled parts of that too.)

"Here." Billie handed me the key.

"Thank you for securing my bicycle."

"I saw the look on your face when you thought your bike was gone, and I said sorry. And you are welcome."

I answered, "Yes, but it didn't last long at all. Now did it? If it had been missing for real, I would have had another case to investigate. Now let's get out of here."

As we walked, Billie tried to bring up boys, but I deflected with the grove and the people and the hives.

Without another word from Billie on the matter of boys, we walked for the next mile in near-complete silence. An uneasy feeling had come over the both of us, but neither could find the words to break the ice. For the time being, it was just as well; we were at the junction where we went our separate ways.

Billie said, "See ya!"

"See ya!"

***

Billie had never felt so alone on the walk home from that junction. What had happened? But she knew. She understood that her friend had nearly immersed herself in the thought of the grove and those people. *But I like boys.* She felt that the other things were excuses to do what she wanted. Billie thought how she had lost her best friend and how lonely she was now. Billie pushed aside a small tear and went on home.

***

I thought of how I could take a look at the grove and be home on time. I decided I would go in today. I would lock the bike to an interior tree out of sight of anyone passing by, not that many people do, but you never know. I thought, *I will only stay a minute or two, have a look around, and then go on home.*

As I neared the spot, I chose to enter the grove, and my heartbeat increased. I could hear the pounding in my ears. I tried to mimic the calm manner my mother seemed to always show.

I am going in anyway, so you might as well get on board, heart, and stop that nonsense. 'Cause I am taking you whether you want to go or not.

That must have worked. Just then I could hear every sound for many yards, and my sense of smell seemed extra acute, and my sight had never been keener.

Bike locked down, I proceeded into the grove.

Next Time, Discovery in the Grove

With a new confidence, I moved ever deeper into the grove. Now unable to see the bike, let alone the road, I determined that there was no turning back now. I stopped for a moment to orient herself.

The bike is in that direction, that tree had a branch removed and it has not fully calloused over yet. I think Lake Josephine is in that direction, Lake Ann that way, and little Hamilton that way. Okay! Keep going. Find the water. It is hard to believe I smelled food from the road before. I must have already traveled a quarter of a mile from the road.

Then just as I passed another row of trees…

"Oh! Look out!"

The words came out automatically from my mouth. But as quickly as the words flowed out, I composed myself, and thought…

It's a rattlesnake eating a squirrel. As long as I don't disturb it, I will not be in any danger. I'll just give it a wide berth and be on my way. Wow! I haven't ever seen a rattler do that before. I've seen water snakes and moccasins eat frogs and fish, but never a rattler eating anything. I love exploring. But it is not the time to explore. I am investigating. I will find out if Negroes live here, in these groves and why they…err if they had something to do with damaging the hives. Smell that? It's not at all the same as what I smelled before. It's awful! I hear sounds, sounds of civilization. Aha! But the lake is still a bit a-ways from here, and I can't be too late getting home. I will have to come back another time to continue this investigation. We have much to load up on the truck tonight for tomorrow's business. Still, I have made progress. I now know the direction to the camp. Back to the bike and home. Where is that snake? There he is, laid out, fat and happy after his meal. I sure am glad I have the bicycle, it gives me some extra time to do things before I get home. I don't want Mother to worry about me.

After retrieving the bike, I flew like the wind and was home soon enough.

I entered the house with a familiar greeting, and this time, there was an answer from the kitchen.

I called out, "Mother! I'm home!"

Mom answered, "I am in the kitchen. Are you hungry?"

"No, ma'am, not very."

Mom replied, "What? Are you ill? Did you have a visitor?"

"No, nothing like that at all."

I said, "I just have a lot on my mind, with the disturbance at the hives, and now I think Billie and I are on the outs…"

"Why are you on the outs?"

"She wanted to talk about boys, and I had…err, I didn't want to talk about boys."

Mom said, "If you didn't want to talk about boys, what did you want to talk about?"

I replied, "Oh! Speaking of what Billie wanted, she said her mom wants a large jar of honey and two black legs on tomorrow. After I finish my snack, may I go to the hives? I want to be sure everything is okay."

Mom answered, "Well, since they do provide for your college fund, it will be okay for you to check on them. But you take the protector." (This was a strong straight oak sapling that Mom used for just about everything, from herding wayward pigs to dispatching unwanted varmints.) "And take your pouches too."

I replied, "Thank you, and I will."

The chores were done it seemed in record time, and being a rural school district, weekend homework was little or none.

"Mother, I'm leaving now."

Mom replied, "Be careful, and don't stay too late. We still have things to load up."

"Okay!"

15

Next Time, Print Seeking

Mother felt confident of my safety since she had already been to the hives and had taken a look around only a short while before I had gotten home from school. She also thought that if I was allowed to explore near our home, I would be less likely to venture off into the groves.

With pouches in pockets and the protector in hand off I went.

I thought, *I will be extra quiet in case someone is out here. I will watch them and find out where they go, then we can call the police and have them arrested.*

Into the woods I went as I neared the first set of hives. A few yards away from the clearing, I looked and listened as intently as I could to see if anyone else was there in the woods. After several minutes, I approached the hives.

Ah! Here we are. Hmm, these are old shoe prints. No new ones. Now I will test my theory. That's odd. Hmm, still no shoe prints even from the other side of the road. I'll go check the next one. I probably will not have time to check them all today, but I will check what I can.

I proceeded to the second set of hives and found the same, no new activity. Then I approached the third set, just as with the two previous sets, stopping and quietly observing from within the confines of the trees and then only after having not seen nor hearing anything, made my way to my destination.

It's the same here also. I guess that is good news. The person has not returned, and we have all of our hives intact. One last thing to check here. Still no tracks from the opposite side of the road. Oh well, it was a thought. But this is odd, what I'm seeing on the road. I had better start back home now. I don't want to be late and the truck has to be loaded still.

The walk back to the house seemed quick; it certainly was uneventful.

"Mother, I am back!"

Mother exited the honey barn carrying two cases of honey.

"Hello, dear, did you find anything new?"

"Yes and no."

"Yes and no? What kind of answer is that?"

"Well, actually I should have said no and yes. You see, I did not find any new footprints at the hives, and I even checked the ground across the road from the hives."

Mother said, "That is good thinking, I didn't even think about that."

I replied, "But I did discover tracks in the road, fresh tire tracks. They could not have been more than half a day old. You were at the hives already, weren't you? And you never got out of the truck."

"Yes I was."

"So why did you let me go?"

"I thought you might find something new, even though you found nothing new of importance. You did think of a new perspective, and you followed up on it."

"I see, for a bit I thought you were just playing with me."

"No, you are a gifted young lady, and I want you to have every opportunity to grow and express yourself. I want you to be who you will be. I don't want you to be me."

"Mother, to be you would be an honor. You provide for all my needs on a daily basis. You have set up a college fund for me. We have a nice home, and we don't owe anyone money."

"I understand what you mean, but it is God that meets our needs. He gives us the way to secure the resources we need."

"Yes, ma'am. At any rate, what do I need to load?"

"Nothing, I am all done. Except for the fresh greens, but those we will load in the morning. I don't want them out overnight. So I left them in the barn."

"I didn't want to be late getting back to help you, so I checked only three sets."

"Don't worry, everything is okay! Even if someone got into the hives again, we can't live out there. I have loaded all I need, and I know you would have helped. I am satisfied with your part. Now enjoy life."

"Mother, you are so wise. Thank you."

The weekend deliveries were as they normally are: productive and uneventful. Except for the tourists who stopped for honey and realized that the gator they bought was loose in the station wagon. What a sight! Good thing the car only ran into a stack of straw hay after everybody had jumped out of it. The gator was corralled, everyone got back into the car, and they drove off.

I waited for Billie, her mom collected her order on her way home after completing errands in town. She simply said Billie will see me tomorrow in church and then she left.

16

Next Time, the Visit (Will It Be a Stranger in the Barn or the People in the Grove?)

Sunday came, we attended church, and Mother socialized a bit afterward with a few of the other ladies. I found out why I didn't see Billie on Saturday for the delivery. Turns out she had her visitor come that morning, and she was ill. She was not her bubbly self, and she didn't want to sit under the oak tree. We kind of just stood and tried to say interesting things, but us two girls could not get that connection back that we had for so long. We said goodbye and just walked away from each other.

It was a quiet ride home, and Mother either had something on her mind, or she felt that I needed to be quiet that day.

***

As we drove on to the property, past the house, all of a sudden, Mother gasped. I looked up at her to see a look of horror. I looked out of the truck in the direction she looked, and I could see the honey barn door opened. There were broken cases in the doorway also. We exited Buck so quickly, I don't even remember opening the door, let alone closing it. To this day, I replay that scene in my mind as though we were those tourists jumping out of their car and leaving it in gear to get away from that gator. I see ole' Buck slowly drive behind us into the barn wall. That's just how it plays out in my mind, though I know it didn't happen that way.

Mother grabbed the protector from the wall next to the barn door. She looked down as she entered the doorway. Glass and honey oozing from the cardboard boxes. She stepped carefully past the broken boxes and through the doorway.

Mom said, "Careful, Debbie, you stay there!"

"Okay!"

I looked at the broken mess, and immediately I noticed something, rather the lack of something.

"Mother, there are no ants, flies, bees, or other insects. This is very fresh!"

I looked around more, tracks going in but not out. Then a loud crash at the back of the barn, the sound of breaking glass. Mother ran back toward me and the doorway. She grabbed me by the forearm (not hurting me at all) and indicated that I should get back into the truck and lock the doors. I did as she said. She moved off a few feet from me and paused just long enough to make sure I did what she had said. She disappeared around the side of the barn. After a moment, Mother returned. The protector in hand and a bit winded, she motioned for me to come to her.

"Did you see anyone, Mother?"

"I got a glimpse of a person running off into the woods. He was covered up pretty good, so I could not see his face. I am sure it was a man, though."

I replied, "I think it was the same person at the hives."

"Perhaps, but right now we have to check the animals and the house, then we will drive down to the hives. I will call the sheriff when we get back. Come with me for now. I want you to stay close to me just in case."

I replied, "I understand! So far I don't see anything else out of place here. He probably went through the barn window 'cause we came home as he was moving the honey out. He saw us or heard us drive up, he dropped the cases and ran to the back. But why? Why run to the back of the barn if you are at the door already? He could just as easily dropped the cases, run through the opened door, and around the back and into the woods. Mother, I think I know who it could be!"

"Who? Who do you think it might be, Debbie? Have you seen someone around here studying the place?"

"No, I have not, but as I think about it, we have never seen the person closely, nor have we seen their face. He is always somehow obscured from our vision. For me the person in the woods was just a shadowy figure moving away. You said you couldn't see him clearly either. Let me ask you this. Could you see the back of his neck or his hair? What about his hands? Were they visible?"

Mom said, "No, no I could not see any part of his body, and he did not seem to turn to look back to see if I was following. I am sure he knew I was after him even though I did not call out for him to stop. It's like he was avoiding me more than evading."

I said, "Mother, I think our undesired visitor is one of the Negroes in the woods."

Mom replied, "Well, we will let the sheriff handle that part of the investigation…all of the animals seem to be okay. There is no sign of forced entry at the house. Let's go check on the hives. But we can't be sure of this. We have not seen one glimpse of this person's skin or face to say it was any particular person, even a colored person."

"So why hide like that? Being so sneaky. Looks like he made more of a mess than a thievery."

"Perhaps we will never know dear. But for right now we have hives to look at, and then we must get back to the business of living. Life goes on in any case, and we will not allow this to set us on a downward spiral."

Mother and I continued the discussion until we reached our destination.

"Nothing looks to be upset here."

Mom replied, "No, it looks like all is well."

I asked, "Aren't you going to stop and look at the hives, Mother?"

"No need. The bees are not agitated. They are moving in and out like normal, and it is obvious no hive is out of place. We have to use our time efficiently."

"Okay then, you drive and I'll spy!"

I replied, "I suppose. Here's the next set. Nothing unusual here either."

"It's just as well. I am tired and a bit peckish."

"Me too! How about fried chicken and potato salad? Some rice and greens and some coleslaw."

I said, "Sounds good to me. What's for dessert?"

Mom answered, "Peach cobbler sounds about right, doesn't it?"

"Mmm! Yes, ma'am! And another one down."

Mom pointed. "Debbie, look there! Wild pigs.

"Uh-oh! I know what that means."

"That's right. We need to do a hunt, so we can keep down the population of feral pigs, or we will lose nearly everything."

"Are you going to call Hoot?"

"I was thinking of it but only as an advisor and safety man. I thought you could head the hunt."

"You know what that makes me?"

"No, what?"

"A head hunterrr!" both said in unison.

Mom said, "Let's get back to the house and see about calling the sheriff and getting some good food."

I replied, "I am with you, ma'am. Drive on, drive on!"

The sheriff, Tom Grady, came out to see for himself, but this was nothing unusual, since there were only two other people on the force. The sheriff and Mother had grown-up around here, so they were no strangers to one another. Mother and I could hear the sheriff's car drive up. She told me to go meet him and bring him to the kitchen, since she was up to her elbows in flour and other fixins.

I said, "Hello, Sheriff Grady. Mother said for you to come with me to the kitchen. She is cooking and can't get away just now."

"Well, hello, Debbie!" the sheriff replied. "You just lead the way."

"The thief sure made a mess of several cases of honey, and he ran when we came home."

"Now hold on for just a bit. Let me talk with your mom first, then we will give you a chance to tell your side of it. Okay?"

"Yes, sir. But I have seen the clues, and I know who did it or rather I have an idea of who did it."

"Yes, yes. But I would like to speak with your mother and make sure she wants me to talk to you about this."

***

Mother greets the sheriff, "Hello, Tom?"

"Hello, Sara. How are you? Was there any personal contact with the vandal? Did either of you get hurt in any way?"

"We both are okay, and we did not get close to the person who did this. I only got a glimpse of him as he ran off toward the north woods."

"Good, good. These incidents are usually the work of vagrants or migrant workers, and unfortunately, we hardly ever catch the ones doing the crime.

Mother answered, "As far as we can tell, there was nothing stolen, just two cases of honey broken. There are several undamaged jars in the cases and a broken window. Although a bit disconcerting, these things happen. Unfortunately, this has happened twice here recently. We had a hive overturned and several others set askew."

The sheriff asked, "Why didn't you report this?"

"I thought it was an isolated incident. Besides, there was no significant damage done."

"I understand, but we could have at least come out to take a report. Even if we did not find a suspect, the person or persons could have been watching. That might have given them pause, and this might not have occurred. Sometimes it's the presence of law that serves to protect rather than apprehending a suspect, 'cause then the crime will have been done rather than prevented."

"All right, I see your point. How about you staying for supper? It is nearly ready, and I suspect that when Debbie tells her point of view you are going to need the energy."

"Nah! I couldn't. I mean, I am on duty, and Deputy Stanley is out sick. So it's just Deputy Frances and me on duty, and Frances, he is manning the phone at the office. Besides I would just have to run out if I got a call, and I would not want to leave all of your good cook'n' on the plate."

Mother replied, "Nonsense, I say! Come on, wash your hands here and have a seat over there. Debbie, please set another place at the table."

"Yes, ma'am. Sheriff Grady, would you like lemon in your sweet tea? Here is a glass of water."

"Thanks, Debbie. Now, Sara you tell me all of it, starting with the first incident. Tell me every aspect of it and then on to this incident from today. Then, Miss Debbie, I want to hear from you. I'm going to just write down what you say, and we will take it from there."

"Sheriff, why do you say we, when it is only you?"

Mother admonished me. "Debbie, that was rude!"

The sheriff replied, "No, no! That is an honest question. When I say we, I am including Officer Stanley who is out sick, yes, and Officer Frances, who is in the office, yes, but more importantly, I am including the law. The law provides the power for me to do what I do. Altogether this makes up the we."

I said, "I see! Even though you are the sheriff, you could not do your job without the help of your men and the power of the law."

"That is right. That is it exactly!"

Mother replied, "Well, here we have a table full of food, and I could not have done it without the power of the stove."

I said, "Oh Mother!"

Sheriff Grady said, "Well, it seems you wielded that power well. This looks and smells wonderful."

Mother replied, "Since you are our guest, I will say the grace. Thank you, Lord for my family, friends, the law, and this food… Amen. Dig in, Tom. If you need something, just ask."

The sheriff replied, "Thanks, but this looks sufficient. Now, if you will, Sara. Give me a recount of events as you are able to."

"Okay, last Wednesday as I went about my normal duties around the property, Hoot contacted me and told me we needed to check the hives. He had felt something. I'll describe it as spiritual. I left a note for Debbie. Hoot and I proceeded to the hives. We were checking for impending swarms and any other issues. Nothing unusual, till Debbie showed up and told us of what she had found."

Next Time, Debbie's Version of What Happened and Who Did It

"Okay, Debbie," the sheriff said, "you've waited very patiently, now you tell me just what you know about the matter."

"Well, Sheriff Grady, it was like Mother said. When I arrived home, she was not here. I found the note in the kitchen with instructions to get some—"

The sheriff interrupted me. "Err, you can skip that part and go to where you were approaching the hives, please."

"All right, as I got close to the first set, I did not see nor hear anything. When I actually got to the first set of hives, I saw that Mother was not there and that all was well with the hives, so I continued to the next set. As I approached, I could hear noises. So as I was taught, I called out to let Mother know I was approaching. It turned out that it was not Mother. When I saw the hives, one was overturned, and several others were pushed around and out of place on the pedestal. I heard a crashing in the woods behind the hives…that would be the north side of the property, Sheriff. I saw what looked like the figure of a man moving off through the trees. I could not make out any features. I found smooth shoe prints on the ground. I left after seeing the tracks to go find Mother."

Sheriff Grady replied, "The bees must have been very agitated. Did you get stung?"

I answered, "No, sir. I was very calm, and I took my time moving in to look. I found Mother at the third set. Hoot was with her. After I told her what I had found, we all got into the truck, checked the other sets just to see if they had been disturbed, and then we went to the set where someone had done their damage. After we set things aright, we went home. Hoot rode with us here to the house, and he walked home from here. Today was as Mother said, we noticed the barn door opened, and we went to check. As I began to tell Mother that the spilled honey had no ants or other bugs, we heard a crash in the rear of the barn. Mother gave chase after she made sure I was safe in the truck. The question is this: why did the person not run out of the opened door when they noticed us coming? Mother said she could not see any parts of the person 'cause they were well covered. The person I saw did not even try to look back to see if anyone was chasing. It is just very odd indeed!"

"Those were very good accounts from the both of you," the sheriff said. "I suggest guard dogs or at least one dog for the place."

Mother said, "Tom, for a guard dog to be effective, it would have to roam free. I can't have a dog biting people or running loose all over the countryside, and tying it up would defeat the purpose of having a guard dog."

"So all you have is me.

"I suppose that is better than having a dog bite someone."

"Tell you what I will do. I will drive by the hives now, and as the days pass, one of us will pass by here from time to time. We will try to make it around the same time as the incidents. Thieves may be bold, but that does not mean they are smart."

"That sounds good, Tom."

The sheriff replied, "Well, I will be heading over to the hives now. Thank you for the wonderful meal. It was delicious."

Mother asked, "Do you want to take some with you?"

The sheriff replied, "Uh, no, thanks."

"Oh, take a plate to Frances," Mother said. "He will like something fresh I am sure."

"Okay," replied the sheriff, "and since you insist, fix a second helping of that cobbler please."

Mother replied, "Okay, just stop by on the way back from the hives."

The sheriff said, "Will do, ma'am…back in a bit."

I asked, "Mother, may I go along with the sheriff?"

Mother replied, "No, you stay here. Okay? Let him do his job. If he needs more information, he will ask."

The sheriff's car could be heard much sooner than it was seen as he returned from checking the hives.

Mother said, "Debbie, help me with these please."

Us two ladies met the car at the back door.

Mother said, "Well, did you find anything interesting, Sheriff?"

"No, no, I didn't. Everything seemed to be in order. But as I said earlier, just the presence of the law can make a big difference sometimes."

"Here you are, hope you and Frances enjoy the meal and dessert."

The sheriff replied, "You didn't!"

Mother answered, "Well, you might get hungry again after you see Frances's plate. Now, if you don't want it…"

Sheriff Grady said, "Ahw! You know I want it. So don't tease me so."

"Sheriff Grady," I asked, "when do you think someone will come by to check on the hives next? 'Cause I want to ride along."

"It will be in two or three days, I suspect, depending on how busy we get. But it is up to your mom if you get to go along for the ride. Okay?"

I answered, "Yes, sir. Mother, will it be okay?"

Mother replied, "We will see what is going on at the time, otherwise it is okay with me. But just once. The sheriff and his deputy don't need you underfoot all the time…understand?"

"Wahoo! Thanks, Mother! Thank you, Sheriff!"

Next Time, the Meeting

The next morning began as most mornings. All the chores were done, then I cleaned up afterward, had breakfast, grabbed my lunch, thanked Mom, and then I was out the door and on the bike and off to school. It wasn't until I had gotten a little ways from home that I realized I had not thought once about my best friend Billie since Sunday. Now I wondered if we would even speak.

Well, I will certainly not ignore her. After all, she had been my best friend all my life. I wonder if she will get to the spot before me. Here we are. No sign of her. No note over here. No note over there. Guess I will wait a while. I hope she is okay. Well, I have to go, it is getting late. I'll just leave her a message over here, it's closest to the direction from which she will come. There! Now, I have to get to school.

No sooner had I secured the bike then the school bell rang.

Where can she be? I really do hope she is okay.

As I walked into the classroom, my eyes fell directly onto the eyes of my best friend. I kind of froze for an instant, not knowing just what to make of this.

No note, and she didn't even wait at the swings for me. What's' going on here?

Neither of us spoke a word to the other all day prior to recess. At the bell...

"Can I talk to you, Billie?" I asked.

"Can you?" Billie replied.

"Okay, may I speak with you?" I asked.

Billie replied, "Yes, I suppose."

"You want to go over to the swings?"

"No, the benches here will do just fine."

"Okay then. Billie, tell me what is wrong. Did I do something to hurt you?"

"Well, if you don't know, I certainly won't tell you!"

"Come on, listen. You and I have been best friends just about all of our lives, and I don't want that to end. Not over a misunderstanding, or something I did wrong, or even an ugly, smelly old boy!"

Billie said, "Even smelly boys can take a bath, and by virtue of the inherent nature of being a boy, he can't be old. Did you do something wrong? Did we have a misunderstanding? I'd say yes to both of the questions. I talked my fool head off about what I thought about boys, and all you could do was talk about those groves and them vagrant coloreds. I thought I was your best friend! Well, best friends talk about everything, not just what one of them wants to talk about! Oh my… Debbie, look! Your visitor is here! Come on, let's get to the restroom. Here, wrap your sweater around you! Didn't you know?"

I answered, "No! I just thought I had a stomach cramp or that something I ate didn't sit well with me. What am I going to do?"

"Don't worry, your best friend is here. I had my visitor over the weekend, so now I carry these. It's not pretty, but you are a woman now. Let's rinse those out, here I have an extra pair. Now put this here, and now you are set."

I asked, "How do you know these things? My mother has never discussed this with me. I just thought these pads were for older women to clean up with."

Billie answered, "My Aunt Myrtle told me about it a month ago."

"But you never told me. Best friends talk about everything, remember?"

"You are right, and I am sorry."

"I am sorry too. And, Billie, you are my best friend! You were here when I needed help."

"No, you got us back to talking again!"

"No, you are my hero!"

"No, you are my hero!"

"No..."

"No...," Billy said.

I replied, "Hey! Let's get out of here... And follow the Yellow Brick Road."

"Okay, but it's red today!"

"Not funny!" I said.

"I'm talking about the Red Clay Road. What did you think I meant?"

19

Next Time, the Meeting Continues

"Here we are, Billie," I said. "Get your stuff out of the basket. Don't forget to write a note on the ground if you get here before me tomorrow."

"Okay, I won't. Hey! Here is your note from this morning. I am glad you did that."

"I am glad you spoke to me again," I said, "and that we are best friends again. See ya!"

"Okay, see ya!"

The journey home this time was not so sad and lonely for either of us this time, but I still had it in my head to investigate the grove and to find out all I could. Not only about the people living there but also about the incidents at the hives and the barn. Being sure it was the people of the grove, I proceeded with as much caution as I could. I left the bike concealed, as before, but this time at the road I left a message wrapped in a piece of plastic wrapper just in case, and as I traveled deeper into the grove I left small pieces of burlap to mark my direction. As I left the pieces of material, I thought, *I wonder who named this stuff burlap? What is burlap? It's not cold, and it certainly does not absorb water well at all, so it does not lap up anything. I like croaker sack much better. I know just what a croaker is. I miss frog gigging with Father. Perhaps I will ask Hoot to go with Mother and me, and we can invite Billie too. Excellent idea! Ah! Here we are. I can't believe it. People really do live out here. Doesn't look like many of them, though. I thought there would be like a tribe, with a chief and all... like on Tarzan. Look there, I wonder what's in that cauldron cooking. That's a pretty good fire under it, looks so hot, I wonder why it don't melt. But I don't smell anything. Oh! A black lady, as real black lady, this is my first black person, a real live honest-to-goodness black lady. She don't look so dark and shiny like I saw on the pictures, but she does have her head wrapped like they do in the pictures and on television. Clothes, she is boiling up clothes. No wonder there was no smells today. Let me just... hmmmm! The pain! For a moment I forgot all about my visitor. I got to get home. Just wait till I tell mother what I saw. Oh no! I can't, I guess the only news I'll be giving her today is that I met a visitor. Billie, I'll tell Billie what I saw. No, I'd better not, 'cause if she tells, then people will come out here and all of my investigation will be ruined. I think I will wait till I get my answers. Well, I am at least certain it was not her that was at the hives and the barn. She is much too large to get through the woods like that person, never mind jumping through a busted window. There has to be menfolk. I'll just watch them for a while and hope to discover the truth.*

"Home again!" I said. "I hadn't even noticed how I got here. Where did the time go? Mother! Mother! Where are you?"

"Out here on the back porch!" Mom answered.

"What are you doing out here?"

"Well, honey, sometimes a person just needs a moment to reflect and get their bearings."

"Oh! I see. Mother!"

"So you finally met your new friend?"

"No! I...oh!" I said. "Yes. How did you know?"

"Honey, I know. Let's get you inside and cleaned up. No chores for you today. It's not quite your birthday, but it is still kind of a new birth. You are a woman now and sooner than you thought."

"Yes, ma'am," I replied. "I thought 'cause my birthday is next week, that's when I would become a woman...because of my age and all."

"Honey, that is only part of becoming a woman. It is only one aspect of what makes up a woman."

"Tell me then just what goes into making up a woman."

"All women are female, all ladies are female. But there are some distinctions between them. They are not born by gender but by learning and choice and by something that is just there inside you. Now there is nothing wrong with the choice a female makes to be a woman or a lady, and to some extent she goes between the choices. A lady carries herself in a good and pleasant manner, but a woman is wise and elegant. She has dignity and sophistication and is able to take care of herself and her family if she has one. She's full of confidence, understands the world at large, and is involved in it. She is gracious and giving. She thinks of others at all times, not just in times of need. It does not matter if she is rich or poor. These characteristics are just some of what makes up a woman, but there are things that are unique to an individual that cannot be defined or fully described. It just comes from within her. Debbie, honey, I see that you are well on your way to becoming a beautiful and confident woman. I am proud of you, and I love you."

"And I love you too, Mother. And I want to be a woman just like you. But Mother, tell me, what is it that caused you to reflect on your life so? You looked a bit sad out on the back porch. Please tell me what is wrong."

"I didn't want to bother you with it," Mother replied, "but I think it is best to talk about it. I miss your father, and I miss having a man around. I miss having the companionship of another adult. Your dad is not away working as I told you. He and I broke up. We are not together because he hurt me. He hurt me a number of times, and he had to leave. So to protect you from that, I made up the story about the job promotion. I don't know where he is.

"Is he ever coming back?" I asked. "Has he written? Did he call?"

"Honey, I don't have the answers you really want. All I know is, I had to protect you. I got the final divorce papers today."

"Oh! Mother, I am sorry. All I could think about was being with Father. Just today I was thinking of how we used to go frog gigging and now this terrible news. But I don't care about me now, all I want is for you to be happy."

"I am a little sad now, but to know you support me is a wonderful help, and that makes me feel much better… Feel like having something to eat?"

"No, but I could use a lot to drink," I replied. "I feel dry as a dirt road in midsummer."

"Okay then! Let's go get something to drink."

"Mother, how long will this last?" I asked.

"All of your adult life. Some women go into their fifties and even sixties but generally till the mid to late forties. It is different with every individual. Now.

"No, I mean for now!" I said.

"Yes, I know what you mean, but I might as well give you 'the rest of the story.' Just starting it may be very erratic, it may go from no show to very heavy, it may be consistent light to heavy. You may just feel a bit upset inside. Your mood may change, one moment you are light and giddy, then the next you may be at your best friend. As for your more immediate concerns, this could last from four to seven days. It just depends on your body. But just starting out, it will likely be spotty and irregular and for only a few days."

"Thanks, Mother," I said. "Another characteristic of a woman is she cleans up well and wears lots of perfume."

"It's not that bad," Mom replied. "But soon, we will talk about when it finally ends later on in life. Did you enjoy the sandwich and cobbler with your drink?"

"I did indeed!"

"You go rest. I have to collect the evening eggs, feed and water the animals."

"But, Mother, I feel fine."

"No buts. You just go and rest a bit, and I will be back in a little while. If you feel like it when I return, we can play chess or checkers."

"That sounds good," I said, "but I prefer reading the Bible some."

"That sounds even better, you can read to me."

"Okay!"

"Back in a bit."

Next Time, the Meeting Concludes; Real Visitors in the Grove

The evening passed with Mom reading the Bible and playing a game of chess. We talked of small, unimportant things. It was as though the both of us had determined to put the weightier things aside for the night.

"Good morning, Mother," I greeted.

"Good morning, dear," Mom said, "did you rest well?"

"I rested fairly well, thanks. And you?"

"I rested well. Are you up to doing the morning chores?"

"Yes, ma'am, I am."

"Okay then go to it. Here is your breakfast."

"I am starving. Thanks."

"I expect the sheriff or Frances will drive by today."

"I hope I am home if one of them does," I said. "I really want to see what it is like to ride in the police car."

"I am sure you will get the chance to ride along with one of them," Mom replied. "Finish up your meal, take care of those chores, and off to school you go."

It seemed that no sooner than it was said that all of the chores were done, and I was on my way out of the door with lunch in hand and a new item to carry along with her salt pouches. The bike ride seemed shorter than usual. Even so, it seemed that Billie had already been there and gone. She had left a message for me. It read, "Been here, but I had to go my best friend has got the flow. Now she is so very slow." I wanted to kill her for that.

"Hey, slowpoke!" (Billie was hiding behind a tree.)

"You had better hide all day, Billie Dean Rogers!" I said. "Come on, let's go!"

"You doing okay today?" Billie asked.

"Yes, and I have my own supplies now. You want yours back?"

"Uh, no. Thanks!"

"I mean a new one to replace the one you gave me, silly Billie!"

"I know what you meant, but it sounded better the way I answered you. Hey! Did the sheriff go by your place?"

"No, not yet," I said. Mother feels someone might come by today. I told her I wanted to be there to go along for the ride."

"Will she let you do that?"

"She said I could go one time."

"Great!" Billie said. "Anything else new going on with you?"

"No, not really," I replied. "Well…look, you keep this to yourself. You hear me? Remember we are best friends, and we said we will tell each other everything, so here goes."

"Okay! I will keep whatever you tell me, to myself, unless you tell me otherwise."

"When I got home yesterday, I saw Mother looking sad," I said. "I didn't want to say anything at first, but I just had to find out just what was the matter with her, and she told me."

A small tear ran down my cheek. "She told me that she and my father had divorced. She had just received the final papers that day."

"Wow! I thought he had gotten a job promotion and was working up north of Gainesville," Billie said.

"So did I until she told me she did that to protect me from hurt," I said. "I guess she figured that if she changed her mind and took him back, I needn't ever know the truth. I felt worse for here than I did for myself, even as bad as things were for me. We had a very long talk about that and about my situation."

"Does any of it make sense to you?"

"I understand most of it I guess," I replied, "but until I experience the rest, I think I will not fully understand."

"I guess," Billy said. "Well, anyway, you know that I am here for you, and if you ever need any help you can call on me."

"Thanks, and by the way, because we are best friends just remember when you are least expecting it—payback!"

"Oh! Debbie, best friends forgive!"

"Perhaps, but they don't forget!

During class, Billie told me that her mom was coming after school to pick her up and take her to the doctor for a routine checkup. I had mixed feelings about going home alone that day, but I realized I had my best friend back, and I was not going to be with her as we usually were, and this made me feel a bit sad. But then on the other hand, because I was alone, I would have more time to investigate in the grove. School ended for the day. Billie and I said our goodbyes and made our promises, and then we went our separate ways. The bike ride was helpful in saving me time, and before I knew it, I was in the grove and slowly walking toward the homestead I had found earlier.

My markers are still in place. Good! Good! They all seem to be here. There! The one of a different color to mark the end of the trail. Now let me see just what they are up to. Smells like food cooking, it doesn't smell bad either. I wonder what it could be? It kinda makes me hungry. There is that lady I saw before, and she is singing. She is singing one of our church songs, but it sounds different. It sounds like she enjoys singing it, as if she were singing it to somebody special. That was so beautiful. But I am not here for food or singing. I have to find out who these people are and if they are involved in the incident at the hives.

"Lill gull! Dat you in dare?" the lady said. "Cum'mone ova hyeah. Let's Beulah mam gits ua good look ats ya. I ain't gonna bite chya, matt'a 'fackly dayes plenty uve food hyeah fo awl 'oe us."

Oh! Goat's feathers, what do I do now? Run…stay? How did she see me? She never even looked my way.

"Dhere won't cum no huarm ta ya lill'un. We be friendly peoples. Cum ohn ova hyeah an let's tawk sum."

"People? What people? Are there more people with her? I don't see anyone else. I think I'll be going now, it is just a bit scary."

I stood up and turned to make a hasty retreat, and standing several feet behind me was a little black boy and a black woman. I was stuck, frozen in place for an instant. I didn't hear a thing, not a sound. I had no idea they were behind me, watching me watch them. She was amazing, so beautiful. Her skin was like black silk, her eyes were like the whitest of white marshmallows, and in the center there had been dropped a shiny black marble. She was taller than any woman I had ever seen before. I had never seen hair like hers before either; it was braided like the mane of the Clydesdale horses and fell to the middle of her back from under a head wrap. The boy was about my age, it seemed. He was taller than she and as thin as the young willows near the lakes. His skin was not nearly as dark as the lady's. It was like the color of a tan pecan or a walnut. He was bare feet and his trousers had been torn at the knee, but they had been mended. They seemed like they intended no harm; at least they didn't try to take me for the pot like I saw them do on television.

"Young lady," the granddaughter asked. "My grandmother asked if you would like to come visit with us and have something to eat and drink. We won't hurt you. We want to know just what you are doing out here in these groves alone. It could be dangerous, with snakes and wild cats on the prowl, a person could get hurt or worse even. Come on with us and set a spell."

"Okay, I will. Now I can't stay very long. I don't want my family worrying about me."

"It is up to you how long you stay. We make no demands of you, we only offer our kindness. Follow me."

Next Time, Talk with the Family

"Hell-o dare, how you is?" Beulah said. "You jist ah inquisitive young thang. Iha wunduhded jist how long you wus gunna spy thu dem trees at us."

"I didn't mean any harm, ma'am."

"Oh, no harm dun, and yah jist call me Ms. Beulah. Dats muha grans dauta Polly, and hur boy Leon. He gunna be a collage graguate sum day and he gonna do fine tings foe people."

"I'm Debbie, I live down the road…"

"We's know wheres you live. Whut uh don't know is why you look'in in on us, and why ya go all da way 'round stead o' cutt'n thru da grove ta git home?"

"Well, for one thing, there are signs posted that says keep out…"

"And yet heah ya be. Go ohn!"

"And my mother said it was not safe to be out here because of you ni…well, because of you people."

"It seems ta me dat you got'ch ya own mind and you gonna do wha'ch ya want anyways. Nut'in wrong wit dat, but you jis know dat dae's consequences to yo choices. Is you ready to pay foe dem choices. I 'spect yo mutha loves ya a lot and she don't want to see nut'in bad come to ya is all. So you do what yo mutha say."

"I am sure she loves me and don't want me hurt. How is it you know where I live?"

"Dees groves is large, but e'men dey gots uh end. When we's git to uh nue place, we's git ta lookin' round ta see jist where we at. Not everyplace we's go is friendly and hospitable. Polly's man saw you at da honey hives. Rat naw we's work'in foe da grove owner trying to git some pesky pigs off'en 'is land. Dem pigs, git ta root'in roung his trees so much dat some of da trees die."

"Tell me, how long have you people been here? At this location?"

"Oh, I spect it been 'bout a mont now. Why you ax me dat?"

"No particular reason. I just wanted to know. I smelled your food and the other stuff you were cooking. The food smelled good, but that other stuff smelled so bad awful that even all of the animals stayed away, it seemed."

"Dat probably wus da soap we wus makin'. Clifford, dat be hur man, caught one u've does pesky pigs and we roasted 'em and rendered da fat. Some u've da fat we keeps for us to use to cook and bake wit and some we use foe us."

"So just what do you use the fat for if you don't cook with it? What smelled so bad that you were cooking?"

"Dat was soap dat you smelded child! We was mak'in lye soap. It good to wash clothes and yo body. We makes two batches, one easy on da body and one ta take de grimiest o' grimes out u've clothes. Dat soap keeps lice and other bugs away too. We make body bham wit sum oe da lard. We takes it and messes it wit some sweet fragrances and let's it steep foe ah li'l while. Afta it dun cools, we puts it in jars. Dats good foe keep'n yo skin smooth an its awlso good foe scrapes and cuts. We sells the abundance from the pigs. We smokes most u've da meat, it keeps that way and den we takes it to where we can sell it. It all foe dat boy rat dere. He goi'n ta be somebody. We gonna send him off ta skool, but he gonna know where he come from. Afoe he go, he gonna kno's haw ta respect peoples, and ah mean all peoples."

"But what about him, doesn't he have a say so in the matter? What if he wants to stay here with his family? Family is very important to us, but it seems to me that you people don't have the same values as we do. I don't know just why in the world you people live out here in these groves!"

"Well, let me ax ya sump'n, den you tell me. Do you s'pose dem pigs gonna come to us in da ciddy, or if we lived in Tampa, ya s'pose dey come ta us dare or we kin git to Tampa an back in ah day wit no cawr?"

"Oooh! So you have to go to where the pigs are, and they are in the groves. You have no transportation, so yo… er you don't move much. And you live on what you can find locally! Yes, I do see! I believe I have enough for now. I must be going."

"Come back anytime you laike and next time, ya eat sump'n. Leon take hur back ta da roawd."

"Do you know what time it is, Miss Beula?"

"Yes, ma'am," Leon replied. "Come on."

"Iah gots no need foe keep'n time. Polly, tell hur what da time is please, huny."

"It is half past…"

"Oh! My gosh, I hadn't realized how much time had passed. Mother will be so very worried and angry with me."

"Lack iah said, you muss pay foe yo choices," Beulah said.

"Grandma, you know if she cut through the grove, she can get home much faster than going the other way," Leon said. "But she'd have to leave her bike."

"Are you sure going through the grove will save me time?"

"Not only that, it will save your bacon, if your mom had a mind to whip you for being late getti'n home."

"Okay then," I said, "I will leave my bike, and I'll pick it up tomorrow on my way to school."

"You gwan nahw and git on home. Leon you make sure she git dare safe. Gwan! Heea, ya take dis soap, it foe yo body and sum o' dis skin bham."

"Thanks, but…"

"Gwan take it and ya git ohn home. We see ta it yo bike stay safe."

"Thank you." *I bet they'll take my bike and sell it like they sell those pigs and soaps.*

"You up for some running?" Leon asked. "That will save you even more time."

"Yes. You lead the way."

"Here, I will carry your stuff," Leon said. "This way."

"So where will you go to school, and who will you live with?" I asked.

"I will stay with family, an aunt and uncle in Tallahassee," Leon replied. "I will finish high school and attend college there. I will decide later on graduate school."

"What will you study in college?"

"Civil law and business.

"Law and business? What has one got to do with the other?"

"You have to understand how to do business to operate your own law firm effectively. I also intend to help others open and operate their own businesses. Do you know that the government gives tax breaks to people who operate their own business?"

"No, I did not know that. What is a tax break?"

"Simply put, the government gives you some of your money back for running your business. If your business is large enough, you can even talk your town or county into giving you tax breaks because you will employ its citizens."

"I guess you becoming a lawyer is to help other Negroes get out of jail?"

"No, it is to help all people, not just colored people, to get the respect they deserve. It is to help them with their rights as citizens."

"I've never heard of such a thing. A colored lawyer, but a colored lawyer starting a business."

"How many colored people do you know then?"

"Uh, none. Except for you, your mom, and Ms. Beulah."

"Kinda my point! And until today you didn't even know us. Look, people may have different skin colors, and they may even speak differently, but they are still people. We meet Spanish-speaking people from Mexico, Brazil, Cuba, Chile, Argentina, and other Latin American counties. And you know what? They have different skin colors too. Some are just as white as you, and some are blacker than the darkest of nights. Like I said, people are people and some need help."

"Good luck! I think I understand it a bit better now. I think you will do it. How do you know all these things now?"

"I learn from people I meet. I go to the library when I can, and I find newspapers and magazines that people throw out. I go to school when we are not moving."

"Hey! Look, there's my place. That's little turtle pond. Cutting through the grove is so much quicker."

"Now that you are home safe, I'll be going back home now. I'll see you tomorrow when you come get your bike."

"Okay, thanks. Bye!"

"Goodbye, Debbie."

"Bye, Leon."

22

Next Time, the Accusation; Who Took the Honey?

I was thinking out loud. "I don't know what all of the fuss is about now. They say don't go into the groves for this reason or that, but there isn't anything to be afraid of in there. Those people are not so bad after all. But I do have this one thing against them: the honey who took it and who was at the hives? It had to be the one person from that family that has been roaming about in those groves all alone—Leon's father. Who else could it be but him! Mother, I am home!"

"Hello, dear! How was your day?"

"Very good! You know, whenever you get to learn something new, it seems to change your perspective on some things and reform your opinion. I met some nice people today. They are not so different from us, except how they live and how they look. Other than that, they have a lot of the same ideas about things as we. Look, they gave me this, some homemade soap and skin balm. I think it is like skin cream."

"That is nice. Did you meet them on the way home from school?"

"I did. Yes, ma'am, I did, and there is this boy named Leon. He is going to go to college someday to be a lawyer and businessman, so he can help other people. I think that is wonderful, that a person could think of others before himself and in such grand terms."

"That's nice, where do they live? I haven't heard of any new families moving in around here lately. What are their names?"

"Uh, hmm, they don't live here, they are Habiru, and are just passing through. Leon's dad hunts hogs for the grove owners. I did not meet him. I met Leon, his mother and his grandmother."

"You mean they are nomads like the ancient Hebrews? Are they nice people?"

"Yes, in a manner they are. They seem to be nice, but I have my suspicion about the father. I think he might be the person who got into the honey. He roams all about those groves and the woods all day. Think about it! Who else could it be if not someone who works in and around the area? I'm suspicious of him all right! The evidence points straight at him!"

"No, dear, he was not the person. The sheriff and his deputies caught the man today."

"They did? Why that's great!"

"Honey, listen to me. Have a seat and let's talk for a bit. Okay?"

"What? What is wrong, Mother? Isn't it a good thing that they caught the person?"

"Honey, the man the sheriff caught…well, there is no other way for me to say this, except to come right out with it. The man is your father! The sheriff believes he was getting ready to burn the hives or even the house today. He bought some gasoline near town, and he was recognized by the station attendant. He told the attendant he was going to do some work around the house, but he would soon be on the road again. The sheriff sent Deputy Frances over to fill up the cruisers, and the station attendant told him who he had just seen, and Deputy Frances told the sheriff. The sheriff got his deputies together and came over here. They found your father with the gasoline out behind the same set of hives he had disturbed before. Honey, I am so very sorry to have to tell you this. But I believe telling you the truth in this matter is best. I tried to protect you from the truth about the divorce, and I felt bad about that, and I felt it did not sit very well with you either, so I am telling you this now rather than later. Besides, you are growing to be a lady, and you need to know the truth."

As the tears silently rolled down my cheeks, Mother and I embraced one another. A small crying moan slipped from me, then my mother cried for me, more so than for her former husband or the disaster that had just been averted. For me, the tears soon stopped, and the hurt turned to anger. Mom realized that I had begun to respond to the situation, and she knew she had to try to prevent me from letting this turn into a bitter hatred.

"Debbie, look," Mom said. "I know it hurts and you loved your father. I love him too, in spite of all that has happened. But you cannot allow this to turn into hatred for him. That hatred will not do him any harm. It will only serve to harm you, and those around you will suffer because of it. So you do whatever you must to get past this and live a good and decent life. Respect yourself and respect others. Do good for people when you can. You do this and things like these, and day by day you will find life will reward you for your effort."

"Mother, I was ready to accuse a man of a crime. A man I had never seen. I feel so bad for that. What should I do about that?"

"We all make mistakes, dear. Fortunately, with some mistakes we can recover. Even though you had clues that led you to believe you had the right person, you simply didn't have all of the facts. Look at this as a lesson learned. After all, you did not make a formal accusation with the authorities. So now you might consider how can you resolve this within yourself? How will you see this person from here on?"

23

Next Time, Confession

"Now tell me who is it you thought got into our hives and barn," Mom said.

"It…he is a colored man. He lives in the grove with his family. The people that gave me the soap and skin balm. They all are colored."

"Deborah Leigh! I have told you to never go into those groves and to stay away from those people. What am I going to do with you? What if they had harmed you out there in those groves?"

"Mother, I am sorry I disobeyed you, but I just had to know who was out there in those groves. I just couldn't help myself. It was like a moth being drawn to a flame. I was compelled to go regardless of the possible dangers. And as it turned out, there was no danger. But I am sorry I disobeyed you, Mother!

"I guess I knew you had seen the colored people; with the soap, and I know there are no new families in the area. I can't be angry with you. I have said in the past, you pray for anyone you like, and if you are going to pray for them, sometimes you have to put some action to your prayers too."

"I just had a thought, Mother. I'll take them a jar of honey tomorrow. I won't mention my suspicion or anything. I will ask God to forgive me tonight for my prayers."

"That is a very good idea. You do that."

"Oh! One more thing I must tell you."

"What is it?"

"I left the bike in the grove, and I cut through the grove to get home faster."

"You walked through there by yourself?"

"No, ma'am. Leon walked with me. In fact, we ran most of the way. His grandma told him to make sure I got home safe. It is so much quicker than coming home on the road."

"You just be careful. I know now that you are going to do as you please. But I trust you."

"I love you, Mother."

24

Next Time, the Gift

As I neared the place in the grove where I left the bike, she could see someone standing several rows back. I recognized Leon and his mom as I neared. I hailed them with a huge wave and big smile, even while increasing my pace. As I entered the stand of trees, I saw them wave back but not approaching the road.

"Hello, you two," I said. "Thanks for bringing my bike."

"Hello, Debbie. I didn't know just when you would arrive, so I asked my mom to come with me to keep me company. Well, here it is. I guess you are heading to school now."

"Yes, and now that I know you, I wish you could come to school with me. But I know that is impossible," I said.

"Like so many things are at the moment," Leon said. "Thanks anyway. Well, you had better be going."

"Yes, you are right, see you. Oh! I almost forgot. Here, a jar of our honey and this is a lucky penny. See how it looks different from this one. I found it in the groves like I found you. I want you to keep it for when you go off to college. One thing I ask is that you don't spend it. I really want you to keep it. I believe that one day you will need the luck it will bring, especially with the schooling you want to have. Promise!"

"I promise. Thank you for your kindness, that means more to me than I can say. Thank you."

Leon extended his hand to shake my hand, and I reached out, and like a magnet my entire body lurched forward, and we both embrace for a brief moment. After a quick and departing glance, we both headed off in different directions.

With new exhilaration, I headed down the road to meet my constant and best friend Billie. I got to the meeting place, and no one was there. I waited like we had planned, and the time came that I had to go. A quick message, simple and straightforward this time. No witty rebuff to Billie's previous prank. A quick glance around to make sure there was no Billie hiding in the trees, then off to school. Still no Billie. The bell rang, and no Billie still. A quick inquiry, and I had my answer—the flu.

The best news I have had in a long time to share with her, and she is done in by the flu. Perhaps I can get Mother to take me to her with some soup. I want to stop by and see Leon and his family too of course. Maybe Mother will agree to meet them too.

The day was otherwise normal. It did to me, however, seem to drag on endlessly. The bell did as always ring at the proper time. The bike ride was full of anticipation and excitement. Finally, I reached the place to enter the grove. No racing heart or voice of warning from Mother. No giant snakes, escaped convicts, not even thoughts of cannibalistic Negroes waiting to take me. Only thoughts of the new friends and the things I would learn.

Odd, no aroma of cooking food or the hideous odor of the soap. No sounds up ahead. What! Gone! The camp is empty! But why? Where did they go?

My mind began to race in all directions at once. Suddenly I felt alone and afraid out there in the groves. A sure sense of dread came over me. Disoriented and confused. I began to head back to the road, and I stopped and started again, but toward the shortcut I stopped and turned again. This time I retreated to the road, and as an automaton I pedaled my way home. Anguish and dread within turned to flowing tears and sadness.

I thought aloud, "He never said, 'See you later.' He did seem a bit sad and a little put off. His mom only said hello and waved. They knew they were leaving. But why didn't they tell me that? I just found a friend and lost him all in the same day it seems. I lost my father. And my best friend is home sick. How much worse can it get?"

"Mother!" I called out.

"Hello, dear," Mom said. "Billie's mother called, Billie is in the hospital. She has pneumonia, and she is pretty bad off."

With tears of overwhelming sadness, I looked to my mother for the only comfort I could find.

"What is wrong, dear?"

"It seems I've lost just about everyone I love in one day."

"What do you mean?"

"Father has gone to jail, Billie is in the hospital, and Leon and his family are gone." I sobbed with a heavy heart because I lost so much all at once.

"Honey, honey, go on let it out. Just cry till you feel better. Go on cry it out."

"I thought it was all going so very well. There were no problems. We live here with no one after us for anything, we have our friends and we are all healthy. Then out of the blue, Father gets arrested for attempted arson, and he is gone for sure. Billie was well the other day. We joked and kidded around, now she is in the hospital fighting for her life, and my new friends. Negroes, the only Negroes I know are gone. And we just met."

"Look, life is full of surprises. Some are good and some are bad. But the thing about it is that no matter what happens there can be some good to come out of it. You just have to look for it most of the time to find it, but sometimes the good, it stares you right in the face and begs you to take him in. Find the good…find the good in all of this, dear. I love you, and I know you will get through this in time."

"How can I find good in Father going to jail? Or Billie being in the hospital, or losing new friends?"

"Like I said, honey, you have to find it. I will give you an example. If your father had set the hives on fire, the woods and groves might have caught on fire too. The good is, we have our bees, and the honey sales will help send you to college. You might not have met your friends if the fire had started, or they could have been blamed for it."

"I see, Mother. Because he was prevented from doing the deed, we don't suffer nor does the grove owners and the people who depend on the work the groves provide."

"You get it, but there is more. There is always more. But you will have to find it yourself, and sometimes it takes time. Just be patient, have faith, and keep looking for your answers. Now let's go see your friend in the hospital."

"Okay. You think they will let us take soup to her?"

"We can certainly try, and if not we can eat it ourselves. But we will offer it to Billie's mother first."

25

Next Time, Conclusion

Thirty-two years later, I'm being interviewed by Carrol Beasley of a nationally known magazine at my home.

Carrol asked what of Billie, the birthday party, my mom, and the boy. I am happy to talk about where they are today and perhaps the time just leading up to now. Billie was doing well enough that the doctors believed she would recover enough to be able to go home in two or three days, and she didn't have to use the oxygen tent. We had to keep our distance, however. Turned out that she never did leave the hospital alive. She not only suffered from pneumonia; she had an aggressive form of cancer. In those days, treatment for either illness alone was problematic. Life was not the same for me after those days. But I kept the encouragement that Mother gave me close to my heart even to this day. Mother was with me well until after my college graduation, a marriage, two grandsons, one great-grandson, and a divorce. I am sure the events of the day helped me formulate the career path I took. I loved to investigate and explore; Leon told me about business and other cultures, Hoot gave me wise insight into nature and life, and Billie helped me understand how friends should trust and respect each other. I miss her so, even to this day.

Oh! Mother and the sheriff got married the year I graduated high school. For an eighty-three-year-old, he still gets around pretty well. What? The birthday? Oh! I nearly forgot that. My fourteenth birthday party, when I became a lady. It was the biggest birthday party I ever had. It would have been even better had Billie been there. But since she couldn't, I had a large picture banner of her made, and I hung it from the ceiling of the church, and we had a double celebration. Everyone thought that was an excellent idea. I still have that picture, and I keep a small one in my wallet.

As I was saying earlier, all this put me on the path I am living today. I became a nurse, then a nurse PhD because I still get to investigate, I have a consulting business, and I give expert testimony in court in regard to medical issues relating to nursing. I am on the medical board of two hospitals and a medical-supply company, I have written one textbook for nurses, and two other books on things I love. I even…uhmm, excuse me. I have to answer the door. One moment please.

"Yes?"

"Deborah Rogers?"

"Not since more than five decades ago! Mills. Debbie Mills."

"Deborah Leigh Rogers was your given name, right?"

"Yes, how may I help you?"

"I am here to thank you for your wonderful gift all those many years ago."

"No! No! It cannot be!"

"Yes! Yes! It most certainly is!"

"Leon! Oh my word! I never thought I'd ever see you again!"

"Yes! Leon Levi Jackson, Esq."

"Come in! Come in! Life has a way of rewarding…"

"Pardon me?"

"I'll explain in time. It just so happens I am telling my story at this very moment, and you are a big part of why I am where I am today. So you are a part of my story. Leon, my interviewer, Carrol. Carrol, Leon, Leon Levi Jackson. I have a full name, and more than that I have my friend back. Mother said if you do diligence and help others as you are able, life will reward you. Tell me, where did you all go and why didn't you say goodbye?"

"Uh, excuse me for interrupting," Carrol said, "but, sir, do you mind if I record this as you two reunite? After all, I am here writing about you both and now that you are here…"

"Leon...please call me Leon, and you continue as you were. It is okay to record me. So many unanswered questions. I will start at the beginning. My dad came home late that night I took you home, he was later than usual. We began to worry, but he finally came home. He was a mess. Some men had beaten him. They said he was trespassing and that he had no rights to be hunting in these woods. There was all of the ugly name-calling and hatred that went along with that kind of wrongful treatment of people. He insisted we pack our things right then and leave. Grandma said no, because we had promised you we would take care of your bike and make sure you got it the next day. He was furious, but Beulah mam had the last say in the matter. She really liked you. She spoke about the 'Lil Whyte Gul' till her last days, and she insisted I find you in time. It took some time, but I found you."

"That you did, indeed! I'm so sorry for that incident. Go on please."

"I am not ashamed to say that I cried all that day. My mom and granny did all they could to make me feel better. And dad, he just said if you got whipped like I just did, then you can cry! We went back to Tampa. Dad got a job doing roofing work, Mom worked in a hospital, and Beulah mam kept house for us. I graduated high school with honors and was able to get a full scholarship for the first four years of my education. I was ready for law school, but I couldn't come up with the money. I had planned to work and go to school at night, but that would add another three and a half years to my studies. At the same time, Mom passed with cancer of the breasts, both were involved. Beulah mam was still with Dad and me, although she couldn't get around, but she remembered the story Mom and I told her about your great gift to me on that last day you and I saw each other. She reminded me I had the lucky penny and that you had said that one day I will need the luck it can bring. So I took that penny, and I was heading over to the fountain at school to make my wish and toss it in when I saw the back of a comic book, and they were talking about rare coins. I took that coin to a professor at school I had become friends with, and he helped me find out about that penny. I am glad you are sitting. Turns out that penny was worth thirty thousand dollars. It is a brass penny, minted during the war when copper and steel were in short supply. There were only a small number that the government never recovered. Deborah, what's wrong? You okay?"

"Yes, and more."

"That penny! Your lucky penny paid for my education!"

"I...I still have mine! I thought about how I found them in the groves and how I found you there too!"

"I had hoped you still had that penny. Did you know about its value?"

"No! I had no clue. Years ago, I had thought to find out more about it, but I was always busy investigating other things, that one day I simply forgot about trying to find out. Besides, it was a special keepsake to remind me of you and our brief meeting and my childhood."

"Like I said, I came here to try and repay your kindness, and I truly am glad you are sitting. Now depending on the condition of the penny and the year, it could be worth several million dollars. The low end, around two hundred fifty thousand. It seems you are not hurting for money, but there are always family and charities. I hope this is good news for you. Another good thing is that I know a pretty fair lawyer who can help you with that if you choose to sell it. Or think of it this way, you invested one of the pennies and the interest has come in."

"Leon, stay for dinner, please. Carrol, git out!"

About the Author

Lee Vern Gadson has, for as long as he could remember, had a longing to tell stories and to know new things. He served twenty years as an enlisted member of the USAF and retired with honor. He began a small plant nursery business in the last two years of service and became a bonsai developer and teacher. After market changes in the local plant economy, he returned to school and trained as a nurse. He served in this capacity for fifteen years.

After retiring from nursing, he increased his bonsai endeavors and began writing unpublished stories and talks.

He tells folks that he served twenty years for his country, fifteen years for his community, and now he is doing this for himself!

CPSIA information can be obtained
at www.ICGtesting.com
Printed in the USA
LVHW091425041020
667875LV00002B/581